CW00486339

A WORKING MOTHER

A WORKING MOTHER

AGNES OWENS

BLOOMSBURY

First published 1994
Copyright © 1994 by Agnes Owens

The moral right of the author has been asserted

Bloomsbury Publishing Ltd,
2 Soho Square, London W1V 5DE

A CIP catalogue record for this book
is available from the British Library

ISBN 0 7475 17142

10 9 8 7 6 5 4 3 2 1

Typeset by Hewer Text Composition Services, Edinburgh
Printed and bound in Great Britain by
Mackays of Chatham PLC, Chatham, Kent

CHAPTER ONE

'I 'll have to get a job,' I said.
My husband replied, 'To get away from me, I suppose.'

'We owe money. The kids need clothes, apart from the fact that we like to eat.'

'Do what you like. I'm tired of carrying you all.'

'You are tired of carrying yourself.'

He nodded. Ten years after the war he still looked as if he had just come home from the battlefield. Flags and bunting had hung from the windows in our street. I had helped to paste the letters reading WELCOME HOME ADAM, and immediately fell in love with his handsome, suffering face when he passed by our window.

'A fine lad,' my dad had said.

'He looks—' My mother broke off.

'Looks what?'

'Unreliable.'

I wanted to run out and touch him.

'Come back from the window, girl,' said my father. Then he ran up the street and shook his hand. The same evening he returned from the pub accompanied by Adam. Both were drunk, but drunk or sober I loved this war hero. Now I wanted to escape from him.

'I think I will go to the city for work,' I said. 'I should get something with no bother. I can type.'

'You're bound to be a success in an office with your laddered stockings and black finger-nails.'

'It's only coal,' I explained. 'I can be smart when I want to.'

'Let's celebrate your new job.'

I emptied my purse and discovered I had enough for a bottle of the sweet, sickly, but lovely South African wine.

*

In a dingy street near the docks I located an agency, to reach which I climbed rickety wooden stairs.

'Could I see the manager?' I asked the young girl behind a window marked Enquiries. Her thin nose quivered.

'You mean Mrs Rossi?'

I nodded.

'I don't know. She might be engaged.'

'Will I come back?'

She sighed and turned down the corner of a page in a paperback on the ledge. 'Wait there,' she said.

Upside down I read the title *Love Came Too Late*. I turned the book round with no real interest and was caught in the act.

'She'll see you,' said the girl, grabbing the paperback.

'It looks good,' I said. She directed me sharply into the presence of Mrs Rossi.

'What is it you want to do, dear?' she asked me.

I sat down. 'Typing, I suppose.' I wondered if there were other possibilities.

'Do you have any legal experience?'

'Actually no—but—'

'It's not important.' She smiled and I was charmed by her eyes shining like two black beads in her plump, olive face. She scribbled something on a piece of paper. I admired the glittering rings embedded in each of her fat fingers. 'You will be fine with this firm. They are very nice. It's a lawyers' office.' She handed me over the paper in a delicate way. 'My commission is minimal,' she said.

'That will be great.' I felt like kissing her hand.

'It's for a fortnight. You can't go wrong.'

3

Leaving the room I collided with the ferret-faced girl on the other side of the door.

*

I located my employers, Chalmers and Stroud, in a street of polished nameplates. My legs dragged up the marble stairs. I had decided to ask if they required a cleaner, but was placed in a large room and seated at a heavy polished table before I could say anything. A kindly-faced old gent entered, shook my hand and said he was very pleased I had managed to come.

'I have no experience of legal work,' I said boldly.

'I'm sure you will manage.'

'It has been a while since I typed.'

'I'm sure typing is like riding a bicycle. You never forget how to do it.'

'I suppose so,' I said, looking at the shelves laden with heavy volumes. 'I can do shorthand too,' I added.

'That's marvellous. You wouldn't like a permanent job by any chance?'

I took so long to answer that he left the room. I closed my eyes in order to relax before I faced the marble stairs again, the bus ride home, then Adam's sneer at my lack of success. The old gent returned with a cup in his hand.

'There's nothing like tea,' he said.

'Thank you, Mr . . .?'

'Mr Robson.'

I drank my tea slowly while he rummaged through a folder.

'Are you finished?' he asked considerately when I had drunk the dregs down to the sugary bit. Then he proceeded to dictate a letter with the words carefully articulated, reminding me of dictation in the primary school.

*

'I've got a job,' I told Adam.

'Good for you. I can now relinquish all responsibility for this household then?'

'And I can save up for a divorce.'

'So, let's celebrate,' said Adam.

*

'Where does Mr Chalmers hang out?' I asked Mr Robson.

'Mainly in the courthouse, to parry and thrust.'

'And Mr Stroud?'

'In a far, far better place.'

He gave me some dictation, during which I could scarcely suppress my yawns, and said at the end of it, 'I like your suit.'

'My husband calls it my Robin Hood outfit.' When he raised his eyebrows I added, 'Being green and kind of merry-like.'

5

'You are happily married then?'

'No.'

'Why is that?'

'Perhaps because my husband was a war hero.'

Mr Robson drew his chair closer to me. 'My wife is dead.' He placed one finger on my hand. 'Of course it happened a long time ago.'

I uncrossed my legs and drew them under my chair. 'That is very sad.'

'I've got used to it.' He coughed then said, 'Of course I don't bother with the opposite sex, but I like listening to their problems. It keeps me'—he smiled wistfully—'young.'

*

'What do you think of old Robson,' a voice hissed in my ear when I was concentrating on an indecipherable word of shorthand. I looked round, surprised at being spoken to by any of the females in the typing pool.

'He's very nice,' I said.

'He's—' The owner of the voice tapped her head.

'Aren't we all?' I smiled shyly.

'Where do you go for lunch?'

'The cheapest place.'

The owner of the voice laughed. Her face was markedly pale in contrast to her short black hair and mascaraed eyelashes as long as spiders' legs.

6

'I know all the cheapest places,' she said.

*

'I lunched with one of the typists today,' I told Adam.

'I hope you're not wasting money on expensive meals.'

'Pie and beans is all I had, besides—'

'Yes, I know, you are earning money.'

'Can I get some sauce?' asked my ten-year-old son Robert, whose hair fell over his eyes in a maddening way.

'We can't afford sauce,' said Adam.

'Where are you going?' I shouted to my eight-year-old daughter Rae when she slithered off her chair.

'For a piss.'

'Don't dare use that word!' But she was gone.

Adam picked morosely at his black-pudding supper. Robert complained that he hated chips without sauce.

'My mother always maintained that meals should be a happy time, a time of unity and serenity,' I said.

'Your mother was a goon,' said Adam.

'She was right about you.'

'Do tell me.'

'She said anyone who was in the war was no use, and the only people who had any guts were conscientious objectors. It took guts to make a stand like that.'

'I don't know about that,' said Adam, picking off some frizzled paper from his black-pudding. 'I saw plenty of guts hanging from trees in the war. They must have belonged to someone.'

'I can't eat no more of this rubbish,' screamed Robert, and ran out of the backdoor.

'Never mind, kid,' said Adam, placing his hand on my shoulder. 'You're doing a great job.'

*

'I never would have taken you for a married woman with children,' said Mr Robson when he had finished his painstaking dictation.

I smiled deprecatingly. 'Especially with all the problems I have.'

'I thought as much,' he said.

'Not that I want to talk about them.'

He patted my knee ever so gently. 'A problem shared is a problem halved.'

'Not with my husband it isn't.'

Mr Robson looked expectant.

After a pause I said, 'He doesn't understand how difficult it is to manage.'

'You mean with money?' His mouth drooped.

'Mainly.'

'You can earn more if you become permanent.'

'I'll think about it, but—it's not only that.'

'Has it'—Mr Robson's voice was hushed—'something to do with the war?'

'I can't talk about it.'

Mr Robson's face became flushed. 'I understand. Perhaps,' he said, taking out his wallet, 'I could advance you something until you get your wages?'

'Oh no, I couldn't,' I said, running out of the room with my pencil and pad.

*

'It's all balls,' said Adam.

'I don't like your language. What is?'

'You out working. The doctor said I was fit to go back to work. How can I, now that you're away all day? Someone's got to be in for the kids coming home from school.'

'Did he write you out another line?'

'Yes—but I don't want to stop in the house for ever.'

I kissed the top of his head where his fine brown hair was becoming thin. 'Take it easy. Your nerves are still shattered from that fireworks display when they opened the new town hall.'

'I couldn't help thinking it was gunfire. I must have dozed off.'

'Never mind, on Friday night we'll celebrate when I get some money. Perhaps we'll see Brendan. He appears to like our company.'

'Which is most unusual,' said Adam.

Much later in the evening the minister on the television said, 'Life after death is something we must contemplate very seriously.'

'I'd much rather contemplate some life before death,' said Adam. He added with a glance in my direction, 'There's not been much of it around recently.'

'Shhh,' I said.

We sat at each end of the settee holding a glass of sweet wine. The kids, protesting violently, were long gone to bed.

'Dying is natural and inevitable,' said the minister.

'Turn that crap off,' said Adam.

'God's ways are mysterious,' said the minister.

'It's peaceful and deep. I like it,' I said.

'I'll give you something peaceful and deep if you come to bed.'

'I'd rather not. I'm much too tired,' I said.

'You're not getting a bit on the side in that bloody office?'

'With Mr Robson?' I tittered. 'He must be sixty if he's a day.'

*

'The streets in the city are so hard,' I told Mr

10

Robson, 'and the soles of my shoes are so thin. I don't know how they are going to last until Friday.'

'We can't have that,' he said, reaching for his wallet.

'It's only a loan—' I began.

'Certainly. Now draw your chair near and tell me more about that poor husband of yours.'

'I have told you about certain experiences during the war.'

'Yes, yes, but tell me how it affected him.'

'You mean mentally?'

He patted me in a fatherly way above the knee. 'I mean sexually.'

*

Hurrying along the crowded streets with Mai, the black-haired typist with the long eyelashes, was exciting, but also demeaning. All the men looked at her, but seldom at me.

'Why do you stare at everyone?' she asked.

'Faces attract me.'

'Only faces?'

'I'm always hoping to see a friendly one.'

'God, you're a scream.'

Whilst munching pies Mai said, 'I wish I could find a nice decent bloke with plenty of money.'

'There isn't any such thing,' I said, staring over Mai's head at a youngish-looking guy

11

with horn-rimmed spectacles. He appeared to be looking at me, but I wasn't sure.

'You mean rich and decent?'

'I mean decent.'

The guy waved. I looked away, just in time. A female rushed past me and joined him.

'Oh well, I'll skip the decent and settle for the rich.' Pointing to the third finger of my left hand she added, 'I see you're married.'

I nodded and managed to swallow a bit of hard crust which stabbed the back of my throat.

'What's wrong? You look upset.'

'Some things can be painful,' I said vaguely.

'You can say that again,' said Mai, slurping her tea and leaving a smear of lipstick on the rim of the cup. 'I was once nearly married but the bastard took cold feet and left me holding the baby. Literally, I mean.'

'What a shame.' I decided that in future I would just take soup.

'It's not a tragedy. Thank God I've got my aunt to baby-sit.'

'With, or without, a husband, it's all the same. I've got two children, and here I am out working.'

'We'd be better off in a kibbutz,' said Mai. There was a smear of tomato sauce on the corner of her lips—it looked like blood. I felt squeamish. 'Can I have those chips?' she asked when I put down my knife and fork. 'As I was saying,' she said between munching, 'that old Robson's a queer hawk, isn't he?'

'He's not bad.'

'I notice he keeps you a long time in his office, yet you don't take long to finish the letters.'

'I'm a fast worker,' I said winking.

She laughed harshly. 'You're a right scream. Wait until I tell them in the office. They all think you're stuck-up.'

*

After that I was popular and included in conversations. I added very little to them, but what I did seemed amusing, and I always winked when Mr Robson buzzed for me.

'The typing pool ladies appear to like me now,' I confided to Mr Robson.

'Who wouldn't,' he said, placing his hand farther up my skirt.

*

'We are doing well for ourselves,' said Adam when I produced some pickled gherkins along with gammon.

'I borrowed some money from one of the women,' I explained, 'and I've got some drink for later.'

The kids looked over. 'Can we get—'

13

'Yeah, yeah, you'll get, when you've finished your meal.'

'Isn't Mummy the greatest,' said Adam.

The gherkins were sour, but the colour contrasted nicely with the gammon and tomatoes.

*

Rain battered on my face on the way to the bus stop. I had no umbrella. I was upset by memories of lost umbrellas. I remembered a particularly nice one. It was mauve with dark-blue flowers—someone had left it on the train so I jumped off at the next stop with the umbrella in the shopping bag before it could be handed in to the lost property. For ages I had wandered around in the rain with a sense of pride. Inevitably I lost it. I don't know where, but I mourned for it like the loss of a friend.

'You're soaked,' said the women in the typing pool. 'Have you no umbrella?'

'I left it in the bus,' I said.

'It happens all the time. Try the lost property.'

'I doubt if it will be handed in. Not many people are honest,' I said.

'You can say that again,' said Mai. 'Someone pinched mine once before I could bat an eye. Expensive it was.'

I looked at her sharply and sneezed.

*

'I see you've got a cold coming on,' said Mr Robson.

'I got soaked this morning. I've lost my umbrella.'

'Poor thing,' said Mr Robson absently. 'By the way,' he added, 'I've an appointment with Mr Chalmers in ten minutes so we'll have to get a move on with the correspondence.'

'Of course, Mr Robson,' I said. 'I just hope I won't be off with this cold. I'm very subject to bronchitis.'

He looked at me slightly taken aback.

CHAPTER TWO

When we were married Adam wore his demob suit. My mother bought me a coat flared from the waist, princess style it was called, and a wide-brimmed hat with a ribbon hanging down the back, but she didn't come to the wedding. In fact no one did, but we wanted it that way.

'Some wedding,' she said. 'A hole-and-corner affair in a registrar's office and not even a best man or bridesmaid. I'm ashamed.'

'Give the lass a break. Besides, it saves bother,' said my father. He was sitting back in the armchair reading a paper with his feet up on a stool, his toes sticking through holes in the socks.

'I haven't even told anyone she's getting married, I'm that ashamed.'

'Leave it be,' said my father. 'It will be all one in the long run.'

16

'Imagine marrying someone that's just come out of jail.'

'He was only drunk,' I said.

'Broke into the post office and was only drunk?' said my mother.

'Stands to reason it was only because he was drunk,' I said. 'He was caught sitting on the post office floor throwing money in the air.'

'Stupid bastard,' said my father. He sniffed. 'Of course I blame the bloody war. They're all nuts.'

'To think I've scrimped to throw her away on a nut case.'

'I'll have to go now, Mum,' I said. 'Do I look all right?'

'You look a bloody treat,' said my father.

My mother burst into tears and handed me a fiver.

*

'He's just gone round for sugar,' said Adam's stepmother, who hated Adam. She leant out of her window, looking down on me from the second-storey flat.

'But he's getting married today. We've arranged it at the registrar's,' I called.

'Oh yes, I believe he mentioned something about it. He shouldn't be long.' She banged down the window.

I waited for twenty minutes outside the building before he showed up. 'Where's the sugar?' I asked. His face looked shrivelled.

'Sugar? I've been for a hair cut. What's that cow been saying?'

'Never mind. We are going to be late.'

'I think this is most unusual,' said the young woman we had approached in the street to ask if she would mind witnessing our marriage.

'It's definitely an honour,' said the young man who had been walking close behind her.

'We didn't want to make a fuss,' I explained.

'Her people don't approve of me,' said Adam.

'It's just that my mother doesn't trust men who were in the war,' I explained.

The couple shook our hands warmly after the short ceremony. They both hoped we would be very happy.

'I have never been so happy,' I said, as we journeyed back in the bus to our lodgings in a room belonging to Adam's stepbrother, who I later discovered also hated Adam. 'Aren't you happy too?' I added.

'I don't know,' he said. Then, 'Sometimes I wish I was back—'

'Back where?'

'Back in the army. I suppose it was hell, but at least it wasn't like this.'

*

Sandwiched between Adam and Brendan in the pub I felt very happy. It was easier to snuggle close to Brendan's bulk than Adam's boniness, though I tried to be impartial.

'Let me pay,' said Brendan.

'It's my turn,' said Adam.

'Bugger both of you,' I said. 'I've just got paid. I'll buy.'

'You're a kept man,' laughed Brendan.

I handed Adam a note and asked him to get the drink. I moved some inches away from Brendan for decency's sake.

'You're looking great,' he said.

'It's just the drink.'

'It isn't. You seem to get better looking all the time.'

Laughing, I patted my hair. 'It's my new hair-do. Underneath it's still the same old boring me.'

'You're never boring,' said Brendan, panting slightly.

Adam returned with the drinks. He looked stern.

'I was just telling Betty she looked great,' said Brendan.

Adam said, 'Hands off.'

Brendan's eyes bulged in his beefy face. 'Sorry, squire.'

'Move up a bit, old fellow,' said Adam, 'you're crushing my wife. She looks unnaturally hot.'

19

Brendan humped along the bench.

'You should have brought a girl friend,' I said.

'I'm not stopping long.'

'Very huffy all of a sudden,' said Adam.

'Not me,' said Brendan, dashing over his drink. He stood up clumsily.

'For God's sake, man,' said Adam, 'you can't leave just like that. I was merely joking.'

'I don't know what's got into you two,' I said, pressing Brendan's foot under the table, 'but if you're both going to be like this I might as well go home.'

Brendan sat down. 'I should have tidied myself up,' he mumbled.

'Tidied up wouldn't suit him, would it, Adam?' I said. 'Being scruffy and nonchalant is his main attraction.'

'Besides he hasn't got anything else to wear,' said Adam.

'I didn't come here to be insulted,' said Brendan, laughing on his way over to the bar to get more drink.

At closing time we all tottered out of the pub. Adam marched on ahead very straight. Brendan's hand had brushed my cheek when he put his arm over my shoulder to hold open the pub door.

'I'd like to do something to you,' he whispered into the back of my neck.

20

We left him standing on the pavement, swaying slightly with his hands in his pockets.

'Bloody pest at times,' said Adam.

'He's your friend, after all,' I said.

*

'There's this fellow who fancies me,' I told Mr Robson, 'and he's a friend of my husband.'

'Does your husband know?' asked Mr Robson.

'He acts as if he's jealous when I'm with them both, but it's just an act. I don't think so.'

'Intriguing,' said Mr Robson. 'Was this fellow in the war?'

'No. That's what I like about him. He's younger than Adam, but anyway I think there's something wrong with him.'

Mr Robson raised his eyebrows.

'Backward. I don't mean retarded, just backward, but he attracts me somehow.'

'Has anything . . . ?'

'Oh no, but when he said that he'd like to do something to me I felt attracted to him.'

'He's not dangerous by any chance?'

'Brendan dangerous? Why he's got the sweetest nature. Mind you, he's a bit uncouth, but he has the most vivid-blue eyes.'

Mr Robson frowned. 'I wouldn't encourage him if I were you.'

'I haven't. It's Adam who encourages him.'

'How's your cold?' asked Mr Robson.

21

'My cold? It didn't come to anything, thank goodness.' I brought out some pound notes from a pocket in my skirt. 'Here's the money I owe you.'

His wrinkled hand closed over mine holding the money. 'Consider this a gift. You're a very sweet person—different from the others, if I may say so.'

After dictating a few short letters he said he was very proud to be the recipient of my confidences since he was writing a book about human behaviour in animals, and perhaps I might care to have tea with him at his semi-detached bungalow the following Sunday.

*

'I wouldn't go if I were you,' said Mai in the café at lunch-time.

'He's harmless,' I said.

'He's a creepy old bastard.'

I bent my head low over my soup. Mai pointed her knife at me.

'I don't get it,' she said. 'It's not natural inviting you out—'

I interrupted, 'It's quite simple. He's writing a book and he wants me to do a bit of typing.'

'Oh yeah?' She leered.

Her face, too close to mine, bothered me. I

22

could see blackheads round her nose. 'You eat too much greasy food,' I said.

'So? What's that got to do with the price of a loaf? I'll say this,' she added, narrowing her eyes. 'He's got bags of money.'

'I'm glad to hear it.' I leaned back, perspiring from the heat of the soup.

'He made his money from the firm years ago. Should have retired, but he likes to nose around.'

'It's up to the firm what he does.' I shut my eyes overpowered by steam.

'They say he's got something on Mr Chalmers —why else would he be kept on?'

'As far as I'm concerned Mr Robson's a nice old man, and if he's going to pay me for doing some typing that's all I'm interested in.'

'You're quite right,' said Mai, and shut her mouth tight. After a minute she opened it. 'I'm fed up with this restaurant. It's stodgy.'

*

Mrs Rossi telephoned me at the typing pool office. 'How are you getting on?' she asked.

'I love it,' I answered.

'And Mr Robson?'

'He's ever so nice.'

'Marvellous,' she purred.

'I might be kept on, but I'm not sure,' I said.

23

'If you make some arrangement come and see me,' she said. The word 'arrangement' lingered in my head like a whiff of orange blossom.

*

On Saturday it rained all day—a heavy torrential downpour with no sign of a break in the sky to allow it to clear up in the evening and give me the excuse for a stroll, if Adam happened to ask where I was going. Brendan and I had arranged to meet on the fringe of the woods—a good twenty-minute walk from the back of our house. With Brendan nothing was a certainty, and with this continual rainfall it was certain he would not be there—but I was compelled to make the effort, being a besotted fool. Adam retired early, worn out by his Friday night binge, which was one thing to be thankful for. I donned an old mac which allowed the rain in as effectively as any other coat, but looked right for it.

'You're going out in this weather?' he asked when I glanced into the bedroom to see how he was.

'I must get some fresh air. All this cooking has given me a sore head.'

'Good luck to you,' he said, reclining against the pillow and viewing me across a library book.

'Perhaps you'd like to come?' I said, banking on there being no chance of it.

'Only fools or lovers would go out in a night like this.' His eyes were steady, but unsuspicious.

'I won't be long,' I assured him, inwardly aghast at my deceit towards this man whom I loved and hated with an equal intensity. Tonight I could easily have loved him, but I loved Brendan so much more. At that moment it seemed conscience does not necessarily make cowards of us all.

I could see a good distance along the path as I walked to the spot where Brendan should be waiting under the trees, though my vision was slightly blurred by the rain assaulting my eyes. I knew he wouldn't be there. Dismally I foresaw myself stumbling through sodden grass in a dripping wood with two pies and a bottle of wine in my bag, but when I reached the tree Brendan stepped from behind it and drew me into his arms.

'Thank God you came,' he said. 'I had no hope you would on a night like this.' He wiped the rain running off my cheeks like tears, adding, 'You must be crazy.'

Hand in hand we picked our way over the spongy grass until we found a patch between some bushes less sodden than everywhere else. I took off my coat (he had none on) and spread it on the ground. He took off his jumper, as rough as steel wool, and rolled it up to make a pillow.

'You'll catch cold,' I said.

'I've already caught it.'

Feverishly we made love, without much sexual satisfaction on my part, but I had the pleasure of making him happy. Afterwards I handed him the wine and a pie. As we ate and passed the bottle between us the rain eased off to a drizzle, but we still shivered in the wet undergrowth. I wondered if I really loved this man, an unemployed labourer, who possessed hardly anything. He was good-looking in a thuggish fashion, but I had seen better-looking—Adam for instance, but then Adam was an old and difficult story.

'Why do I love you, I wonder?' I asked Brendan.

'God knows,' he answered, wiping his mouth on the back of his hand as he finished off the pie. He replaced the cross and chain round his neck inside his jumper. It had been dangling in my face all the time he was on top of me.

'You're going to get ulcers one day,' I said.

'Who cares about one day. Today is what matters.'

I nodded. Perhaps it was his freedom I envied. It was on the tip of my tongue to say that it would be better if we didn't see one another again, when he asked, 'How's the big fellow?'

'Adam's fine,' I replied, angered and insulted by the question. 'Why do you ask?'

He shrugged. 'My conscience maybe.'

I jeered. 'So, afterwards your conscience bothers you, but never before.'

He didn't answer, but held his hand out for the bottle.

'You don't really love me. You just use me.' I was falling into the old trap again, just when I had the notion to break loose.

He gripped my arm, making me wince. 'I love you, I love you, I'll make a record of it, and send it to you so that when I'm dead and buried you can play it over and over, if that's what you want to hear.' He looked at me miserably and I was glad to have wrung the words out of him. He added, 'But sometimes love has nothing to do with it.'

I eased out the cross from under his jumper. 'Has it to do with this? Some pagan superstition, I suppose.'

He drew back as if I'd slapped him. 'I don't think so.'

Gently I took the bottle from him, satisfied I had hurt him. I drank a mouthful of wine and understood what Adam meant when he once said that it tasted as good as chocolate. The

27

sun shone through the trees for a second, then vanished.

Brendan groaned. 'Don't tell me that it's going to clear up now that I've caught my death lying in this mud.'

'That's your precious God's way of doing things. Give them a taste of how it could be when it's too late.'

He grinned. 'Better late than never. At least I will have died making you happy.'

'Of course,' I retorted, 'you only make love to me out of the kindness of your heart.'

'One time you are going to make me hit you,' he said, gripping my wrist hard. I wished then he would hit me so that I could have more power over him.

'You make it sound as though it is pure hell for you being with me.'

'Most of the time it is,' he said.

'I wouldn't worry too much if I were you. You can always confess before we meet again.'

Perhaps I had gone too far. He said coldly, 'What makes you think we will meet again,' and rose to his feet.

When I stood up he helped me on with my very wet and crumpled raincoat. I found a damp handkerchief in my pocket and wiped the leaves and mud from his horrifying pull-over and in turn he wiped my coat. We held hands again as we waded through the grass to reach the point of separation. We regarded each other sadly.

'I'll probably see you around,' he said.

I forced myself to smile. 'You know it's impossible to escape me.'

I ran back down the muddy path wondering if I might be the victim of some lurking maniac, and also thinking resentfully that if Brendan really loved me he would not have let me return by this sinister path on my own.

*

'I said that will be all for the time being.'

Mr Robson's cooing voice brought me back to the uneasy realisation that his ten minutes of dictation had been receiving scant attention from me.

'Be careful with that report. It's for the head office,' he added darkly.

'Yes, certainly,' I said, but thought, 'You'll be lucky.'

CHAPTER THREE

When war broke out I was thirteen years old. I was on holiday with my parents in an unspectacular seaside resort. The only thing I liked about it was the small window on the sloping attic roof above my bed. Everything else was boredom: long walks with my parents, sitting in a deck-chair beside my parents, watching my parents play bowls in the bowling-green set aside for visitors behind the church hall. I heard about the war from a conversation between my mother and the landlady, who was frying some ham for our breakfast. I was sitting in the toilet separated from the kitchenette by a thin wall when I heard my mother shout on my father. A radio was turned up and I stopped feeling bored. Quickly I flushed the toilet and joined them.

'Shall we all get killed?' I asked.

The landlady, who was ancient and wore a man's cap, put her finger to her lips as the three of them continued to listen to the sonorous voice of the newsreader. They appeared frightened. I left the kitchen and went upstairs to my parents' room. I took a ten-shilling note from the purse in my mother's handbag then returned to the kitchen. They were still listening to the radio in fearful concentration. I noticed the ham on the gas ring was frizzled.

'Can I go out to play?' I asked loudly.

My mother made a vague gesture with her hand as if to say clear off. I wandered into the main street and purchased twelve chocolate liqueurs from a distracted woman in the sweet shop. On a bench on the promenade I ate two of the liqueurs, feeling excited and slightly drunk. Apart from being sick I cannot remember much of the remainder of that day, except for my mother saying to my father as I went to my bed under the sloping window, 'I am positive I had another ten-shilling note. I wouldn't be surprised if that landlady pinched it while we were out.'

Later on I remember looking up at the red sky through the attic window and associating its splendour with the seven and six I had left in my knickers' pocket.

*

'You knew nothing about the war,' Adam was saying.

'I knew about Sidi Barrani, El Alamein and Tobruk. When we went to the Saturday matinée the names went through my head all the time like the dreary poems you got at school. Then there were the Desert Rats. We were hoping to see big rats in the sand. All we saw were tanks and guns. We used to stamp our feet and shout, "We want James Cagney. Give us the picture." '

'While men were dying,' said Adam.

'You didn't die. I wish you had.'

'So do I when I look at you and these brats and this dump.'

I smashed my empty glass into the empty fire-place. 'Don't dare call my children brats. Call me what you like, but not them. They are innocent.'

'Innocent—that's a laugh. They could teach the Arab kids a few tricks.'

'You'll know all about the Arab kids. Penny for my sister—'

'I'm going home,' said Brendan. 'I can't stand this.'

'Don't go,' said Adam and I almost simultaneously. 'We're not really fighting.'

'No, stay,' said Adam. 'I'll get another bottle. We'll be all right with another bottle.'

I raked in my bag and threw him some money. 'Don't be long and don't drink any before you get back.'

32

'Unlike you, I've got some decency,' he said, leaving the room.

'I can't stand when you argue like that—it does something to my brain,' said Brendan.

'I know,' I said, holding his head to my chest and stroking his hair. It was as tough as wire.

'Adam is my friend,' said Brendan, nuzzling closer.

'And I'm your friend too,' I said. 'We'd better be quick. He'll be running down the street.'

'What's the matter with him?' said Adam when he returned and was unwrapping the brown paper from the bottle.

Brendan was weeping in the chair.

'It's because we were arguing,' I said. 'He can't stand it. It does something to his brain.'

'Come on old chap,' said Adam, putting his hand on Brendan's broad shoulder. 'We won't argue again. We're pals now, Betty and I. We're all pals.'

In a low voice he hissed to me, 'See what you've done.'

*

My first meeting with Brendan had been one Saturday afternoon when Adam brought him back to the house after the pubs closed. He had the friendly look of a brigand from a Mexican film: swarthy, unshaven, and too young to be a war veteran. I perched on the arm of the chair where he sat and accepted a glass of cheap wine from his bottle.

'Meet the wife, Brendan,' said Adam.

Brendan's hand when he shook mine was strong and warm, the smile on his broad face with its flattened nose had melancholy charm, and I noticed his eyes, unlike a Mexican bandit's, were vividly blue. He didn't say much. Adam entertained us with some humorous war experiences I had heard before. The kids came in and hovered near Brendan. My son Robert studied the label on the wine bottle and asked Adam if he could have a sip, at which question I slapped him on the ear. He immediately howled, and my daughter kicked Adam's leg for the hell of it. It would have been a bad moment but for Brendan, who produced two separate shillings for them. They ran off, delighted. After that I put on a record called 'One Enchanted Evening'. Brendan and I waltzed, or rather shuffled around the floor, while Adam sat with downcast head, silently crying, which was a bad sign. Not long after that Adam had Brendan by the throat and was pushing him towards the door. Brendan's powerful hands unlocked Adam's rather easily I thought. He pushed Adam back on the chair and punched him on the mouth. Adam wiped his mouth and looked vacantly at the blood on his fingers.

'It's the war,' I said. 'It's affected his brain, especially when he's drinking.'

'Are you all right?' said Brendan, wiping Adam's lip with the bottom of his pullover, which was ripped.

'I'm sorry,' said Adam, pulling on a bit of wool and unravelling it even farther. 'I didn't mean it. You of all people, my friend.'

He broke down again and Brendan cried too. I went into the kitchenette and made some tea.

*

'So you see,' I said to Mr Robson, 'Brendan has almost become part of the family. The kids call him Uncle Brendan.'

'Children invariably adopt acquaintances of the parents as relatives. It is a sign of insecurity,' he stated in a lofty manner.

'My children are very insecure,' I agreed.

'It seems to me this Brendan is also insecure.'

'Indeed he is. Being insecure myself I have noticed how much more insecure he is. He has no employment to speak of, apart from an odd gardening job here and there, because he feels so insecure.'

'Perhaps he's just lazy.'

'Oh no. Brendan would do anything for

35

anybody. If you met him you'd know what I mean.'

'H'm,' said Mr Robson. After a pause he said, 'Has he become your lover yet?'

'It's hard to think of Brendan as a lover. We are seldom alone together except for one time when Adam ran down the street for a bottle of wine. But to be honest I don't really want to be alone with Brendan for too long. He has no conversation.'

'It all sounds very intriguing,' said Mr Robson.

*

On Friday evening after leaving my employment I took a jaunt to the dock area to visit Mrs Rossi. The office girl raised her eyebrows when she saw me.

'Well,' she said.

'I would like to see Mrs Rossi, if you don't mind,' I said, staring her out. After a long pause she inclined her head towards Mrs Rossi's office. I could have sworn there was a smirk on her lips.

'You've come at a bad time,' said Mrs Rossi, stubbing a cigarette into a saucerful of ash. 'However.' She shrugged.

'It's nothing really,' I began. 'I just want to ask your advice.'

'Advice?'

'But if you're busy—' I said.

'I can spare ten minutes.' She lit a cigarette and looked at me enquiringly.

'I have been offered a permanent position with Chalmers and Stroud and I wondered—'

'Well that's just fine, dear.' Delicately she blew a smoke ring into the air, a study in sophistication. Her black earrings matched her black eyes and contrasted well with her bejewelled hands.

'I hate being tied down,' I said.

'Tell me,' she asked, 'are you a Gemini?'

'Come to think of it, I am.'

'Geminis are like that—always on the move, easily dissatisfied, but often very talented.'

'Fancy that,' I said.

'You've got me going now,' she said, casting the papers on the table to one side. Then she brought out a pack of cards from a drawer and dealt out six of them face downwards. One by one she turned them over with great concentration. I scarcely breathed. She closed her eyes for so long I thought she had dozed off. I coughed nervously. Her eyes when opened were so black she appeared to have no irises.

'There are three men in your life,' she said, 'one of whom you have great doubts about. Cast your doubts aside, for this man is good for you and he will improve your circumstances greatly.'

37

I asked timidly, 'Does this mean I should stay on at Chalmers and Stroud?'

'Oh dear me,' she laughed, looking quite normal now. 'You'll have to make up your own mind about that. I can only convey a general impression from the cards. Any elaboration could be misleading.'

'You have been most helpful, Mrs Rossi. It's been very interesting to discover you can tell fortunes.'

'I don't do it in a big way, just now and then when I get the urge. Come and see me again. Who knows, I might get another urge.' She laughed unusually loudly.

The office girl shoved her ferret face round the door asking, 'Did you shout?' and looking at me suspiciously.

'Yes,' said Mrs Rossi, suddenly appearing hostile. 'There are letters for posting. Get a move on with them.'

'Good-bye,' I said, heading for the door, but neither of them answered.

*

'Tells fortunes!' exclaimed Mai as we sat pressed close at the table of McFenny's Food Service Cafeteria, which we were sampling for a change. 'Sounds dodgy to me,' she added.

'Everyone sounds dodgy to you,' I said, trying

38

to get some spaghetti to my mouth with my right elbow wedged in her side.

'There's a lot of dodgy people around and I consider fortune tellers are very dodgy.'

'She's not a professional, just reads the cards when she gets the urge.'

'Gets the urge?' Mai repeated giggling. 'This spaghetti's marvellous, isn't it.'

'It's very long. They should cut it up in smaller pieces. It reminds me of worms.'

Mai dropped her fork. 'You've put me off. I can't take another bit.'

'It's disgusting anyway.'

We sipped our tea with heads close to the cups.

'Honest to Christ, I'm really fed up with everything,' she burst out.

'Sorry,' I said.

'I don't mean the spaghetti—just everything.'

'How's that?'

'I can't go on like this, forever sitting in with the baby all week then going to the dancing on a Saturday and meeting no one, no one that's interesting, that is.'

I shrugged. 'At least you go to the dancing.'

'What do you do on Saturday nights—watch the telly?'

'Actually I go out for a drink with Adam and his pal Brendan, and leave the kids to the telly.'

Her head swivelled round. 'Brendan, eh. What's he like?'

'He's hard to explain. You wouldn't like him.'

'Try me. Three's a crowd, four's company.' Her eyes were pleading.

'It's a good distance. Oh well,' I said, 'I'll give you the name of the pub and directions later in the week, if you want.'

'Marvellous,' she said, and clapped her hands.

*

'Did you know that Geminis are always on the move, easily dissatisfied and often talented?' I asked Adam.

'No.'

'According to Mrs Rossi they are.'

'Who's Mrs Rossi?'

'The woman who runs the agency.'

We sat round the table looking down on burnt mince.

'I hate mince,' said my son.

'I hate burnt mince,' said my daughter, and banged her spoon down on the plate with a dollop of mince stuck to it like cement.

'It's not easy to burn mince,' I told Adam.

'I fell asleep. I'm always tired nowadays.'

'Doing what?' I shoved a lump of rock-like substance in my mouth. When I got no reply I went on, 'Anyway, between Mrs Rossi saying that Geminis are talented and Mr Robson wanting me to come to his house on Sunday and do some typing for him—for which I will get paid extra—I am quite pleased with myself.'

'I'm glad you're pleased, because we're not—are we, son?' he said to Robert, who was by this time staring at his meal with intense hatred.

'So go and take a banana!' I screamed, at the same time catching hold of Rae, who was sliding down her chair to escape. 'And you, miss, don't move!'

All was ominously silent for five minutes. Then Adam said, 'Next week I'm going back to work and you can stay at home.' He picked up Robert's banana skin from the table and threw it at me shouting, 'This definitely can't go on.'

'You forget,' I said, catching the skin, 'that you were sacked last week by post, so it will have to go on, and furthermore I will be going out on Sunday to earn some more money.'

'Can we come with you?' said Rae, who had been in a fit of giggles over the banana skin.

'I'll take you both out on Saturday, to the seaside perhaps, if you're good.'

'Is Daddy coming?' asked Robert.

'Of course he is, if he's good.' I put my arm round Adam's shoulder. He now sat slumped with his mouth moving strangely. 'Won't that

41

be a good idea,' I said, 'to get away from everything.'

'Is Uncle Brendan coming?' asked Rae.

'Uncle Brendan has no decent suit to put on. Besides he once said he didn't like the sea. It makes him want to drown himself.'

'I'll come,' said Adam, shaking his head. 'I'll come and drown myself instead.'

'It will be nice,' I said, patting the back of his fist lying clenched on the table, 'for the four of us to have a trip by ourselves for a change.'

*

'Betty is taking us to the seaside,' Adam told Brendan in the pub on Friday, while my eyes were glued on the door looking for Mai.

'That will be nice,' said Brendan.

'Sorry old chap, it's just me and her and the kids. It was her idea.'

Brendan recoiled and wiped his mouth as if it was all crumbs. 'Of course. I wasn't suggesting. I mean I wouldn't intrude on a family outing.'

'Especially you not being one of the family and not possessing a decent suit even,' said Adam.

Brendan looked down at his pullover, which looked as if it had been knitted with black rope. 'Bit of a mess,' he said ruefully, 'but I'm getting some new gear from my mother's catalogue.'

He added sadly, 'Can't stand new clothes. They never fit me.'

'It's not that, Brendan,' I said. 'You told me once you hated the sea. I didn't think you'd want to come.'

He blinked. 'That's true. I don't really like the sea. Can't remember much about it though. Don't know if I was ever at the sea. I don't think I should like it,' he added hastily, giving me one of his vivid-blue stares.

'Come if you want to,' I said casually. 'Oh look,' I shouted. 'Here comes my friend Mai from the office.'

She was pushing her way through a crowd near the door wearing a purple dress and a black hat with gold metal buttons round the brim.

'There you are,' she said all breathless and sportive. Her mouth fell open when I introduced her to Brendan. She simpered at Adam, saying, 'I've heard a lot about you.'

'You have?'

'Nothing but the sweetest things,' she said. She was like an actress in a silent film except for the sounds she was making.

'Can I get you a drink?' said Adam in a dignified way which made me proud. Brendan looked flushed and worried. I squeezed his hand behind Mai's back.

'Get us all a drink,' I said loudly, 'so we can all get drunk.'

Brendan laughed as if it was a great joke I had made.

'Isn't she terrible,' said Mai waving her hands about. 'That's why I like her though.'

When we were seated Mai sat between me and Adam. Brendan was on my other side. By the slant of him he appeared to have half a buttock on the seat.

'Move over,' I said. 'Brendan's arse is not the size of a pygmy's.'

Adam's nostrils distended. He does not like me being coarse in company.

'I'm fine,' said Brendan, holding on to the table for support. Mai and I were jammed as close as Siamese twins, and the fumes from her perfume seeped through my pores.

'Hope you don't mind me coming,' she hissed into my ear, reinforcing the vapours.

'I'm glad you came,' I said.

Brendan from his position half over the table called across to Mai, 'Any friend of Betty's is a friend of mine.' I could feel the heat from his flushed face.

'Er—yerrs.' She turned to Adam and said something, to which I saw him stiffly nod.

For the rest of the evening Mai spoke to Adam between the drinks that were ordered by me, Brendan and Adam, but never by Mai. I couldn't hear what they were saying and when I did look enquiringly at Adam his eyes were

44

downcast on the floor. Brendan said, 'Your friend is very lively,' and I jabbed him hard in the side. After that he said nothing. The drink seemed to be having very little effect on me, so when we got up to leave I was surprised to find I could scarcely stand. I grabbed the table to steady myself and discovered I was alone. Brendan was waiting outside, Adam and Mai were arm-in-arm moving onwards.

'They're a couple of bastards,' I said, clutching Brendan's arm.

'I don't like her much,' he said. 'She didn't say one word to me all night.'

'You weren't missing anything.'

'You're a lot better looking than her,' said Brendan.

Now I felt more steady and sure of myself. 'Let's walk along by the river and let them do whatever they want to do.'

'Are you sure?' said Brendan.

'Sure I'm sure. I don't want to go back to the house and find them banging each other on the floor or up against the wall.'

'Adam's not like that.'

'You don't know him,' I said darkly.

*

When I got home three quarters of an hour later, Adam was in bed.

'Where did you disappear to?' he asked.

45

'Looking for you,' I said. 'I went to the toilet and when I got outside you'd all disappeared.'

'What happened to Brendan?'

'How should I know? What's more to the point, what happened to Mai?'

'Her?' he said. 'I was never so glad to get rid of anyone in all my life. I made sure she got on a bus right away.'

'So you say,' I said, taking off my shoes and surprised to see that they were thick with mud.

'I just hope Brendan's OK,' he said before turning round for sleep.

'Who cares?' I said, feeling sick.

CHAPTER FOUR

O n Saturday morning I lay in bed as long as I could, praying for rain while Adam snored. I consider him an attractive man, although he no longer attracts me, but when he snores I have an intense aversion for him. I long for a bed of my own. Rae burst through the door.

'Mummy, get up. It's all sunny and you said you would take us to the seaside.'

Adam sprung up as if he'd been spattered by grapeshot. 'What is it—what's happening?'

'We are going to the seaside,' I said joylessly. I arose and shuffled downstairs to face the litter of yesterday's unwashed dishes. It was incredible how much litter could gather in one small house in one day. It would have been simpler to burn the place down and start afresh, but the insurance policy had run out. By the time I had washed up and made toast and marmalade Adam was stumbling around the kitchenette, displaying a bleeding chin from a blunt razor blade while he searched dementedly for his tie.

'Perhaps you strangled Mai with it,' I suggested.

'Who is Mai?' he said, emptying out a pile of dirty linen on the floor.

'It's all right, Daddy,' said Robert triumphantly. 'I found it under your bed. It's all stinky.'

We had a sniff at the tie and came to the conclusion the smell was stale alcohol.

'Just put it on,' I said. 'It gives you a certain aura.'

One hour later we were as ready as possible to leave when we discovered we had lost the key.

'We can't go until we find it,' said Adam.

'Let's forget it then. We won't bother going.'

The kids wailed, stamped their feet and punched the wall.

'All right, we'll go,' said Adam. 'Anyone that breaks in will die of fright.'

'There's only the record player that's worth taking,' I said.

'It's broken anyway,' said Rae.

Outside the house we peered about, our eyes dazzled with the sun.

'I could do with a drink,' said Adam.

'Better not,' I said, watching the kids sprint

48

along the road. 'The train could be due any minute.'

We waited in the station for fifteen minutes before the train left. The kids hopped in and out of the toilets and scampered close to the edge of the platform.

'You never realise how much you detest your kids until you take them somewhere,' said Adam.

'I used to hate going places with my parents when I was a kid,' I said. 'We should be glad they want to come with us.'

'From what I can remember of your parents I don't blame you.'

'At least they gave me a sense of security. Our kids don't have any.'

'For Christ's sake,' Adam shouted, 'I don't know where you get your ideas from—'

The train slid into the platform and we rushed on like lemmings heading for oblivion.

*

Later, with our backs resting against the shore wall, Adam and I drank small sips from a bottle purchased from the licensed grocer's.

'I suppose it was worth it,' said Adam.

'I knew it would be nice.'

'Yes nice, an apt description—reminds me of your mother somehow.'

I stared at the silhouettes of the kids poised

49

on the rocks far in the distance. 'I've always liked being on the beach,' I said.

'I was on the beach once—for three months, trapped. I didn't appreciate it much.'

'Don't let's talk about the war,' I said, 'not now.'

'Sorry.'

I let the sand trickle through my fingers. A wind sprang up and I shivered.

'Have a drink,' said Adam.

I reached for my cardigan. 'Why does everything remind you of the war?' I asked.

'It was the only time I felt alive.'

'So you enjoyed it.'

'You wouldn't understand,' said Adam. His eyes stared towards the horizon like a castaway.

I snatched up the bottle saying, 'I've never made you happy, have I?'

'I'm happy enough.' He sounded uninterested.

'Me too,' I said, appreciating the heat of the liquor reaching my stomach.

He rose to his feet and headed towards the rocks, then scrambled up beside the kids and pointed seawards. They all stood still like totem poles. I closed my eyes and was disturbed by the recollection of Mr Robson and the book he was writing. It didn't seem right. Afterwards we wandered through a park high on a hill behind the town. We sat on a wooden bench behind some bushes and munched doughnuts washed down with lemonade for the kids and sips of alcohol for Adam and me. A blanket of cloud dimmed the sun.

'It's been a nice day,' I said, possessed by an urge to leave.

'Very nice,' said Adam, with the sly look of one who knows better.

'What's wrong?' I asked.

'Everything's perfect.'

Robert ran over with a pair of sunglasses he had found. I put them on.

'How do I look?' I said. The rims were broken and the perspex cracked.

'Like a film star,' said Adam. He handed me the bottle saying, 'Finish it off.' When I put the bottle to my lips he said, 'Watch out. Here come the bizzies.' It was only a doddering old park keeper, who gave me a strange look when he passed.

'We'll have to be going,' I said.

The kids made sounds of agony. 'Just when we were enjoying ourselves!'

'That's the best time to leave,' said Adam.

'Perhaps we should stay a while longer,' I said. 'It's still early.'

'I want to go home now,' Rae snarled. 'I'm fed up.'

Adam laughed as if he had heard a joke. The effect of the alcohol lay like a tight band on my head. I placed the empty bottle in a litter bin and walked away from them. The journey back in the train was passed in silence. The kids looked sullen and disappointed. I closed my eyes to blot out their faces.

*

Brendan turned up on our doorstep at nine o'clock in the evening, holding a black bottle and bulging out of a grey pin-stripe suit.

'You're a sight for sore eyes,' said Adam.

Brendan looked down at his legs. 'It's not too tight is it?'

'You look terrific,' I said. 'Like a business executive.'

'More like a top Mafia man,' said Adam.

'Mafia?' repeated Brendan.

'Have you never watched Mafia films?' said Adam. 'They all dress like city slickers.'

'It's from my mother's catalogue—delivered this morning. Did you go to the seaside then?'

'Yes, and we had a lovely time,' I said.

'You should have come,' said Adam.

'I thought about it, only—'

'Why didn't you,' I said, pouring wine into glasses.

'Can I sit on your knee?' said Rae, dashing in and tugging Brendan's jacket.

52

'Get away,' I screamed. 'Your fingers are all jam.'

Brendan stood in the centre of the room with a beautiful soporific smile on his face while we all admired him. After the subject of his appearance was exhausted I asked him how his mother was keeping.

'Fine,' he said uneasily, adding, 'She thinks I should look for work, now I've got this suit to pay for.'

'What about a factory,' I suggested.

'I wouldn't advise working in a factory,' said Adam. 'It's too claustrophobic.'

'I don't like being indoors—except in pubs or houses when I'm drinking,' said Brendan, winking at Robert who was still admiring him.

'A building site then,' I said.

'H'm,' said Brendan. 'I worked in one for a few hours. The ganger kept shouting and swearing at me. I wanted to hit him with my shovel, but I just walked away instead.'

'You should be a bank robber,' said Robert. 'That's the best thing to be. That's what I'm going to be.'

Brendan ruffled his hair. 'Good idea. We'll be partners in bank robbing when you get older.'

'What about the gardening work? You're good at that,' said Adam.

Brendan nodded. 'Don't mind digging gardens. The last place I was at the woman was always asking me in to fix things. I got fed up.'

'Fix what kind of things?' I asked.

'Like plugs or taps and things. I'm no use at fixing things,' he said, turning away as if to drop the subject.

'Maybe she wanted you to fix her,' said Adam with a guffaw.

'Brendan could fix anybody if he wanted to,' said Robert, looking fiercely at his father.

'You two kids—off to bed,' said Adam, gesturing with his thumb in a menacing manner.

'Sure would like to fix a lot of people,' said Brendan, giving me one of his vivid glances.

Next morning I slept almost to midday. I remembered too late about my appointment with Mr Robson. The effort of dressing was too much bother. I slopped around in my dressing-gown listening to Nat King Cole records and handing out coffee and cheese sandwiches as a sop to dispirited appetites. Brendan lay on the sofa most of the day looking like a whale cast up to die. At four o'clock he rose and left us without a word. Three hours later he returned with bottles of booze. I don't know how he manages it.

*

On Monday morning I didn't want to rise. I didn't want to cook the breakfast, or go to

54

Chalmers and Stroud, or see Mr Robson, or lunch with Mai. I wanted to sleep until I was tired of it, then rise and sip coffee and eat rolls, then stroll through the park and sit when I felt like it or walk when I felt like it. I wanted to be alone and free.

'Time to get up,' said Adam, turning off the alarm.

'Yes, darling,' I said in tones of loathing. 'Do you want one slice of toast or two?'

'Nothing,' he said.

I dressed furtively with my back to him.

'By the way,' he said, 'I shall be gone when you get back.'

'Will you, darling?' I said, adjusting my suspender belt.

'I can't stand you anymore.'

'I'm not surprised,' I said, feverishly looking through a drawer for a blouse which would certainly need to be ironed.

'Why is it,' he said, 'you always try to drag me down when there's an audience?'

'I wouldn't call Brendan an audience.' I viewed a crumpled blue article with extreme despondency.

'What would you call him then?' He sat bolt upright against the pillow. In a brief glance I noticed he looked slightly deranged.

'A half-wit,' I answered.

'In all my experience—' he began.

'Would that include the war?' I said sarcastically, hoping to shut him up.

'I've never met anyone as chilling as you.'

'What did I do?'

'What did you do?' he laughed. 'What did you do? It would take all morning to describe what you did—laughing, crying, kissing Brendan, the poor fellow was completely confused—and screaming how I'd never been anywhere during the war, that is anywhere farther than Aldershot—'

'I'm sorry I can't stop to hear all this, I've got to work you know.'

'So I'll be gone soon. I can't take any more.'

*

'Sorry I'm late,' I said to Mr Robson, smoothing down my crumpled blouse. 'I've had a terrible week-end.'

'Dear, dear,' he said. He was reaching up for a book on one of the shelves called *The Joys and Fears of Extra-Marital Bliss*.

'I thought I wasn't going to make it this morning,' I added.

He opened the book at a particular page, studied it for a moment, then closed it. 'What happened?' he asked.

'It's my husband's friend Brendan.' I paused, folding my hands and looking blankly ahead. Mr Robson gave a barely perceptible nod as if he could anticipate something ominous in connection with Brendan. 'The last time we saw him, which was on Saturday night, he appeared slightly deranged, and—' I paused again.

'Yes?' Mr Robson tapped his fingers on the table, then coughed.

'He accused my husband Adam of being a fraud. He said he knew for a fact that Adam had never been farther than Aldershot during the war because he had spoken to someone who had known Adam when he was in the army. This person had told Brendan that because of Adam's high degree of intelligence they had kept him in a special unit to decode enemy communications.'

'It all sounds very commendable,' said Mr Robson.

'When Adam heard this he nearly took a stroke. He was literally foaming at the mouth with rage. He tried to strangle Brendan, who fortunately has a strong, thick neck and came to no harm, but Adam was in a bad way all day Sunday; that's why I couldn't manage to come to your house. He paced about swearing vengeance on Brendan, saying over and over again that he had been a complete dumb-cluck during the war; that's why he'd been sent abroad to fight and die for his country along with a million other dumb-clucks. I said I believed him, but now I'm not sure. He is very intelligent you know.'

Mr Robson puckered his bottom lip with his fingers. 'I must say the situation has taken a strange turn, but it sounds to me as if it is your husband who has acted in a deranged manner.'

'That's where you are wrong,' I said. 'It was predictable that Adam would act like that under the stress of Brendan's accusation. But for Brendan to make the accusation is completely out of character. I doubt if he has even heard of Aldershot, and even if he had it would be beyond him to concoct such a story.'

'Then,' said Mr Robson with a sigh of impatience, 'he has spoken to someone who knew Adam during the war, as he said.'

'It's hard to say.'

Mr Robson opened his book again and peered hard at the writing as if looking for a solution, or perhaps a distraction from my network of probabilities.

'I hesitate to say this,' I said shyly, 'but do you think Brendan could have a split personality?'

Mr Robson looked up and opened his eyes wide, showing his milky irises. 'That would be beyond my judgement, but'—he smiled in his fatherly way—'do you know what I think?'

'What, Mr Robson?'

'I think it all boils down to sex. It's all in this book you know, the lengths a person will go to when he or she is foiled by a member of the opposite sex for whom they have a great desire.'

'Sex?' I repeated.

'It is obvious that they are both jealous of each other because of you. Animals are much more direct. They fight it out straight away and the best animal wins. Brendan and your husband are complex humans who have no idea what they are about. Human behaviour, my dear'—he squeezed my hand which lay listlessly on the table—'is very complicated.'

*

'You were in old Robson's room a long time this morning,' Mai hissed into my ear when I was placidly typing my rather dull correspondence. 'It's getting beyond a joke.'

'What are you talking about?'

She shrugged and gestured backwards with her thumb. 'It's them. You know what they're like. They see bad in everything.'

I regarded the assortment of females sitting at their desks in casual attitudes of employment. 'Perhaps I should leave,' I said.

'I didn't mean that,' she said as I brushed past her to stop at the desk of a very nice

59

woman called Miss Benson, who had confided to me recently how worried she was about her nephew who was doing badly at university.

'Tell me,' I asked her in a voice audible to everyone, 'do you really want me to leave?'

She threw up her hands as if I was holding a pistol to her head. 'Why should I want you to leave?'

'It has come to my ears there is a lot of talk about the length of time I spend in Mr Robson's room taking dictation, which does not appear to be justified by the amount he gives me. Well,' I continued in my very audible voice, 'this is because he spends most of the time reading his mail before he replies to it.' From the corner of my eye I saw Mai creep out of the office. I continued, 'What seemed a joke at first is getting beyond a joke, or so I'm told.' I waved my hands in a despairing fashion. 'Perhaps it's better I should leave.'

After a minute's silence the females twisted and turned in their seats and looked at each other with concern, then at me with concern. Mrs Grimble, a fat, homely female who had been with the firm for thirty years or so and who, according to Mai, had no time for Mr Robson, having described him as an overbearing old fool, said, 'My dear, I think this is too utterly ridiculous, and I for one would like to make it known that if anyone is suggesting there is some sort of—er—'

'Hanky-panky?' said Miss Partridge, a young-ish typist who sat behind Mrs Grimble.

Mrs Grimble frowned. 'Don't be offensive. What I mean to say is if we're going to make something out of the amount of time that is spent over Mr Robson's dictation then I think we're all potty.'

'Exactly,' said Miss Benson. She gently led me back to my desk, saying, 'I don't know what to make of people nowadays. Before the war everyone was much kinder. Now they have no sense of decency. I blame it on the cinema.'

'I would simply hate Mr Robson to have any inkling of—' I broke off and sat down shakily. 'He's such a kind man.'

*

Mai was unnaturally subdued at lunch-time when we sat on stools, side by side in the new Wimpy Coffee Bar.

'It's a lot dearer in here,' I said.

'Yes.' She chewed half-heartedly on her beef-burger.

'Appetising though.'

'Yes.'

'Not hungry?' I asked.

She put down her beefburger on the plate.

61

'You didn't have to make such a commotion this morning. I was really embarrassed.'

'And how do you think I felt? I mean if people are going to tittle-tattle what am I supposed to do?'

'You exaggerate everything,' she said, having another go at her beefburger.

'I'm a very sensitive person.'

She gave me a black look from her blackened eyes. 'You're so sensitive it isn't real.'

I laughed and said, 'Did you enjoy yourself on Friday?'

'It was all right,' she said. 'That Brendan looks a proper weirdo.'

'I hope you're not going to start talking about my friends.'

'Sorree. I'd better watch it, hadn't I, otherwise you'll be leaving again.'

'I can't go through the same act twice in the one day,' I pointed out.

'God, you're a scream,' she said, tucking into the remainder of her beefburger.

'It's strange that you didn't take to Brendan. He's the sweetest person really,' I said. 'He's not a weirdo at all, otherwise we wouldn't bother with him. I mean if you're going to judge people by the clothes they wear or how charming they appear you're easily impressed.'

'I just don't fancy him, that's all. Matter of fact he gave me the creeps,' said Mai.

'Have you ever noticed his eyes?'

'No,' she said, leaning back and giving out an unbecoming belch. 'Though it sounds as if you fancy him.'

'Brendan's not the type one fancies. He's someone you can rely upon when the chips are down. That's why I admire him.'

Mai blew through her lips as if it was all beyond her understanding. 'I must say I much prefer your husband, not that I fancy him either. And even if I did, I wouldn't encourage him. I don't believe in encouraging married men; it's not fair to the family.'

'I don't care if you encourage him or not,' I said coldly. 'I haven't found him attractive for years.' Distastefully I stared around the Wimpy Bar. 'Considering the prices they charge in here it's extremely dingy. I don't think we should come back.'

She raised her heavily pencilled eyebrows. 'What do you expect for two and sixpence? The Imperial Hotel or something?'

I closed my eyes to blot out the sight of her offended, moon-shaped face. 'I expect to get value for my money.'

We left the Wimpy Bar yards apart. Outside we became parallel.

'I don't feel so good,' she said. 'I don't know what's wrong with me nowadays.'

I looked at her with a touch of pity. 'I've noticed your breath smells bad. I didn't want to say, but remarks are being passed in the office. Perhaps you are eating too much greasy food, or perhaps it's constipation. I'll say this much for Brendan. He might be a weirdo but his breath doesn't smell.'

*

At home Adam and I sat at the table by the window looking outwards, which was preferable to looking inwards. The room was a riot of dust and clothes scattered around like empty cushions.

I said, 'Do you know, I believe that Mr Robson is a Jew. Do you know why I think that?'

'No,' he said.

'Because for one thing he has a big aquiline nose and his eyes are very dark brown.'

'H'm,' said Adam.

'I never noticed this before, probably because being kind of old and white-haired you don't notice much about him. Though I suspect Robson could be a Jewish name.'

'For Christ's sake!' said Adam angrily.

'I hope he pays me. I mean you can never tell with Jews.'

'Pays for what?'

Wearily I said, 'He wants me out to his house

this Sunday to do some typing. I was supposed to go last week, but I couldn't be bothered.'

'Who's going to make the Sunday dinner?' said Adam, his interest snapping to attention.

'Can't you make it on a Sunday for once? It will only be for you and the kids. Probably I'll get something at Mr Robson's.'

'For once!' said Adam, staring wild-eyed at the kids, who were throwing stones over the fence at the cat next door. He banged on the window, then turned to me still wild-eyed. 'I can't stand Jews.'

'You can't mean that,' I gasped. 'After all they've suffered it's blasphemy!'

'Don't start on about what they've suffered because it doesn't mean I have to like every Tom, Dick and Harry of a Jew who asks my wife out to some penthouse for supposed typing and is up to God knows what.'

'Penthouse!' I laughed.

'Apartment, bungalow or mansion, it's all one. You're not going.'

'I don't understand you,' I said, at the same time hearing the man next door call the kids a couple of sadistic little bastards. 'You didn't bother too much when I told you before. Is it because he's a Jew next?' I became angry. 'Is that what it is?'

The kids clashed by the window, laughing. Adam banged his fist on the table, then stood

65

up and towered over me with hands on his hips, reminding me of my father's intensive inquisitions when I was a child and he was about to thrash me. I stood up also to be in a less vulnerable position. We faced each other with what amounted to bared teeth.

'I am going anyway,' I said. 'We need the money.'

'So,' his voice sank, 'you need the money, and with a Jew too. It has come to this.'

'You're completely mad. I'm going to do a bit of typing for an old man who is writing a book called "The Study of Human Behaviour in Animals", and who probably isn't a Jew. It was only supposition.'

'Animals? By God that's rich. Who the hell is he to study anything? Does he experiment on them as well, does he?' he shouted as he shook me vigorously.

Robert ran in and kicked Adam on the shin. 'Leave my mum alone,' he ordered.

'Big pig,' shouted Rae at his back.

Adam sat down. He looked exhausted. 'Please yourself,' he said weakly. He explained to his attackers, 'It's all her fault. She prattles on a lot of shit about Jews and animal behaviour. She's trying to drive me crazy. What do you think, kids?' He smiled pathetically. 'Do you think she's trying to get me into a nuthouse?'

Robert turned on me. 'Don't talk any more

66

shit to Daddy. Anybody that's been in the war can't stand it. Leave him alone.'

'What time's Uncle Brendan coming?' asked Rae. 'He doesn't talk shit, does he, Daddy?'

*

'I'll just leave things the way they are,' I told Mrs Rossi after she remarked that I looked distraught and did I want a transfer. At this point the office girl, whose name was Poppy, came in with a pot of coffee on a silver tray that also contained a silver milk jug and sugar bowl. Two fine cups and saucers were already on the table.

'It's just that I didn't want to feel tied down.' I had been explaining about Mr Robson.

'You need to have an escape route?' she asked. 'Is that it?'

'An escape route? Yes—well—I see what you mean. I wouldn't say that exactly.'

'Everyone should have an escape route,' she said in her unfathomable way. 'Do you like my silver?'

'It's lovely—so elegant.'

'It's from Poland—the Germans would have loved it, even though they have no flare for elegance.'

'I thought you were Italian. You look Italian.'

'Fortunately I do, and to make it appear a certainty I married an Italian soldier who was with a German unit. He also thought I was an

Italian.' She laughed in her heartless fashion. 'He never found out. He was blown to bits by a bomb placed in an army truck by the Polish resistance, which was a great relief to me. All the same, he was my escape route.'

'You've had an exciting life,' I said, filled with uneasy admiration for this resourceful woman.

'It's all very placid now.' She sighed as if regretting life's placidity.

'My life's very boring. I long for some excitement,' I said, sipping the coffee and liking its nutty flavour. 'This coffee is excellent,' I added.

'It's only Maxwell House instant,' she said. 'Shall we have a look at the cards, then?'

She studied the cards she dealt out with all the intensity of a scientist studying life through a microscope. The hairs on the back of my neck rose. Then she picked up one and said, her face rigid and unfamiliar, 'Beware of a dark-haired man. He means you harm.'

Adam, Brendan, they were both dark-haired, and Mr Robson undoubtedly had been dark-haired before he turned white. Did that count, I wondered. Which one of them meant me harm? Perhaps I had not met this particular dark-haired man.

'How can you tell?' I asked.

She picked up another card without looking at it and waved it in front of my nose. 'You will evade this harm because this card

68

denotes there is a force for good on your side.'

I received this information with boredom, since it amounted to nothing. The next card apparently conveyed that there was money involved somewhere, but it was difficult to say if it was to my benefit. I sensed Mrs Rossi was losing her power when she rubbed her eyes and yawned. The card she now showed me was the ace of spades.

'Death?' I asked.

'Not necessarily,' she said, 'but I can go no farther. Sometimes it has to do with persons themselves. It's hard to tell.'

'Perhaps it's the cards.'

'No,' she said, boxing the cards and returning them to the drawer. 'It's never the cards.'

'I'm sorry,' I began.

'Not at all, my dear.' Her eyes looked puffy. 'We can't expect results all the time.'

At that point Poppy entered and told Mrs Rossi there was someone for her on the outer telephone.

'How annoying,' she said, giving me a look of regret.

'I'm going anyway,' I said, rising.

'Don't forget to call on me if you have any problems.'

CHAPTER FIVE

'I don't want you to have anything to do with these Yanks,' my mother used to warn me. It was the fourth year of the war and I was sixteen, all dolled up and ready to head to the amusement arcade with my pal.

'I hate Yanks,' I said, which was only part true. I liked their thick, drawling accent, their ochre-coloured skin and their brashness. I didn't know what brashness meant in those days, but their eyes embarrassed me, as all-knowing as if they could see through to my bra padded with bits of cotton wool. My pal appeared quite at ease as they watched her play the pin-ball machine while I stood by her side drooping with self-consciousness. I wanted to be noticed by them but if they did happen to give me a sidelong glance I flushed up like a chameleon. My pal's strident laugh at everything they said was a challenge I could not match with my feeble, forced titter.

'Regular little sad apple,' said one of them contemptuously, when he spied me mooning over his black slicked-back hair and black moustache reminiscent of Clark Gable. I turned my usual beetroot red, then walked away from them to hide my distress.

'Where are you going?' my pal yelled.

I turned and stuck my tongue out. 'Big Ears,' I called, since the Yank also shared that feature with Mr Gable.

She caught up with me. 'What's wrong with you?'

'I wouldn't be seen dead with these Yanks,' I said. 'They would rape you as soon as look at you.' I wasn't sure what the word 'rape' meant in those days, but I sensed it was about the worst thing that could happen. However, when my dad brought two of them home from the pub one evening I was quite happy to loll around with one leg over the arm of a chair and view their gratitude at being seated round the dining table, which was an old-fashioned kitchen effort varnished over. Surprisingly my mother gave them a plate of spam sandwiches and Dad opened bottles of beer.

'It must be terrible, being such a long way from home,' my mother said to them, at the same time pushing my leg down.

'We're only too happy to be here,' said the small one with slant eyes, who had introduced himself as Aza. The other one, who had told us to call him Buster, beamed all round the room, saying, 'Gee whiz what a swell little place—what swell folks,' and guzzled down his beer in two gulps. My mother brought forth a bottle of port from the sideboard drawer and gave everyone a drink from the small crystal sherry glasses she only used at the New Year—everyone except me. When she left the room and returned minus her wrap-over apron I poured and drank a half cupful of it before she could notice. I immediately felt groggy, hot and cheerful. It came to me that this Aza one was very attractive, and I was possessed with an urge to kiss his thin, manly lips.

'Where's the er—' He gestured backwards with his thumb.

'You mean the bog,' said my father, leering.

My mother tutted and led Aza out of the room. It seemed they were gone a long time. When my mother returned I saw her hair was dishevelled and her lipstick smudged. I think I was the only one who noticed. Buster was wolfing down sandwiches while my father talked about the battle front like one who has inside information. I saw my mother in a new and unpleasant light. With her knitted V-neck jumper drawn tightly over her big chest, and her short tweed skirt clinging to her pot belly, she looked as sluttish as Mary Kelly from down the street, who walked about squiffily arm-in-arm with anyone in uniform. I darted out of the room and collided with Aza who was buttoning up his fly. He gripped my arm, pushed me up against the wall of our hall (as mother called it) and shoved his hand up my skirt. For a split second I had quite a pleasant sensation before I was sick over his tunic. In the next second I saw his face turn ugly before I ran into the toilet and was sick again down the pan. Five minutes later, when my mother barged in and said, 'Have you been at the port?' I was on my knees retching. Finally I stood up and faced her, water streaming from my eyes, relieved to see she looked like my normal waspish-faced mother again.

'That American tried to rape me,' I told her.

'The dirty bastard,' she said. I went straight to bed and fell asleep to the sound of abuse coming from the kitchen.

*

'During the war an American soldier asked me to marry him,' I told Mr Robson in a moment of abstraction.

'Perhaps it was wise that you didn't,' he said. We were drinking our morning tea drowsily. The heat from the radiator plus the heat from the sun streaming through the glass pane was clouding my brain.

'Shall I open a window?' I asked.

'Afraid it is not possible. The window cord has snapped.'

'It is so hot in here,' I said.

'I find it very comfortable,' he said with a touch of asperity.

I stifled a yawn, saying, 'Perhaps it's just the way I feel.'

'It can't be the menopause yet,' he laughed, his leathery skin lying in folds round his neck like a chamois cloth. I shuddered at the word menopause.

'Hardly,' I said, my voice cracking a bit.

He tapped my knee in his fatherly way. 'You were saying about this American?'

'I wish I had married him. People are much better off in America. But my mother wouldn't allow me because I was too young.'

'Being better off isn't everything,' said Mr Robson reprovingly.

'I suppose not.' My eyes drifted to his pin-striped shirt, red satin tie and gold tie-pin. I sighed. 'It wasn't meant to be.'

'It's interesting that you say that,' he said, lighting a cigar. I closed my eyes to appreciate better the aroma from Havana. It suggested golden sands, drifting canoes and the magic name Copacabana.

74

'What did I say?' I had a compelling urge to place my head on his shoulder and sleep.

'It wasn't meant to be.' He shook my arm. 'Wake up, my dear. I believe I'll have to turn this radiator off after all. Now,' he said after he had done so and sat down again, 'you should not believe that things were either meant or not meant to be. It is a superstitious attitude and not worthy of your intelligence.'

'Perhaps I'm not intelligent then,' I said.

'Of course you are, otherwise we would not be discussing such matters. It is the intelligence and awareness in your eyes that appeal to me.'

'Really?' I sat up straight, widening my gaze.

'You'—his forefinger stabbed a bone in my chest—'are the master of your fate. It's up to you to decide whether events are meant to be or not.'

'I don't see how I can alter anything,' I snapped. 'It's so bloody difficult—'

'Tsk, tsk,' he exclaimed gently. 'Perhaps I could help. Visit me on Sunday and we shall discuss things at greater length.'

'What about the typing of your book?'

'That too.' He added, 'My house is an Aladdin's cave—full of treasures.'

*

'I'll have to skip going for lunch today,' I explained to Mai.

'Oh,' she said. 'Hope it was nothing I said.'

'Don't be stupid. I've got to buy something—' I waved my hands about. 'I'll have no time to eat.'

Her stupid, accusing face twitched. 'I could come with you.'

'It's not possible.' I turned my back and called out to Miss Benson, 'How is Andrew doing now?' That was the name of her nephew in the university, who was of no interest to me.

'I think he's settling down to his studies again,' she began.

'That's marvellous.' I flashed her a sympathetic smile and listened to her long enough to dispatch Mai from my side. 'I hope I haven't made an enemy of Mai,' I interrupted Miss Benson.

'Why do you say that?' she asked, dropping the subject of her nephew like a hot potato.

'She is beginning to take over my life,' I said plaintively.

'She's a funny one,' said Miss Benson. 'Doesn't really belong here. She uses far too much make-up for an office.'

*

When I returned home in the evening Rae tugged my coat before I could take if off and said the teacher wanted to see me to discuss her work at school, then Robert informed me

76

that he had torn his jacket and would I sew it right away, and Adam stated that we had run out of potatoes. Wearily I sat down and said I was thinking of packing in my work because everything was getting on top of me—added to the fact that Mr Robson expected me to go to his house and do typing for him, but since I couldn't stand the strain of the row it would cause I'd better leave.

'And then what?' said Adam.

'What do you mean—then what?'

He shrugged, smoothed down his hair. 'How will we manage?'

'You can sign on the dole like everyone else. We're bound to survive.'

'What's the dole?' Robert asked.

'It's a big building where they hand out money.'

'I don't believe that,' said Rae, 'or else why didn't we go before?'

'You have to be very poor and unable to work, and they only give you enough to buy bread and corned beef and wear old clothes and shoes from a rag store.'

'Cut it out,' said Adam. 'Don't listen to her. If your mother wants to pack her job in, I'll get one—don't worry.'

'I'm glad to hear it,' I said. 'In the meantime is there anything to eat?'

'There are some old bits of gammon and a few squashed tomatoes,' said Adam.

'If you look properly you will find sausages in the cupboard. Do you think you could manage to cook them? We can have bread and sausage at least. In the meantime I am going to lie down on the settee.'

Rae woke me up later with the meal and a pot of tea on a tray. 'Daddy thinks you should go to work,' she stated.

'Why should I?'

The thick sandwiches were excellent and the tea most refreshing.

'Because we need sweeties,' she explained.

'Perhaps you'd better keep working meanwhile,' said Adam, 'but come next Monday I'll look in at the paper-mill. They're bound to start me—'

'So in the meantime I've to carry on whether I like it or not—'

'No one is forcing you. Do what you like—'

'Exactly. That's what I'll do.'

I retreated to the bathroom to spend some time applying what make-up I could lay my hands on.

'Going somewhere?' asked Adam, when I passed him on the stairs.

'I have arranged to visit my friend Mai,' I said on the spur of the moment. I had no intention of visiting her. It was just an excuse.

'You mean that one—'

'Yes, that one.'

'I didn't like the look of her—'

'I don't like the look of your pal Brendan. I have to put up with him just the same. Make sure the kids are in bed before I get back.'

'You're not leaving me with the kids again?' said Adam, aghast.

'For God's sake, they're your kids too!'

'I can't stand another minute of them.'

'No doubt Brendan will come round and comfort you in your hour of need.'

'At least let me have the price of a drink.'

Thin-lipped I put some money on the table and departed with what I hoped was an air of purpose. Outside I gave a fleeting thought to Mr Robson's address, but prudently decided not to go there. After all, it wasn't Sunday. I waited at the bus stop unsure of what to do. When a bus came along I jumped on with a feeling of relief and sat down beside a fat, jolly lady, who immediately opened up a conversation on the peccadillos of buses and bus drivers, which I listened to with a deep sense of appreciation. This was replaced by a sense of dismay when I had to get off at the terminus. The jolly lady turned round and waved me good-bye. I was forced to walk away smartly to create a good impression. In actual fact I didn't know where I was going. I wandered around for twenty minutes, avoiding the glances of lonely males cruising the city aimlessly like tourists in a non-conducted outing. Master of my fate indeed, I sneered to myself. One nod of the head to any of those wayfarers and I could finish up floating along the city river face downwards. Heedlessly and needlessly I had blown good money on bus fares when I could have been at home sharing Adam's bottle in the discomfort of my own home. Then it came to me that I had Mai's address in my jacket pocket. With something like joy I brought out the scrap of paper and there it was: M Paterson, 12 Angelio Street. I liked the name Angelio. It sounded romantic.

It turned out that she lived in the top flat of a three-storey dark and dingy building reminiscent of the apartment we shared with Adam's stepbrother in the early years of our marriage. The title of 'Mrs' was on the nameplate to fool the neighbours, no doubt, and likely fooled no one. She took a while answering the door, though I knew she was in. I could hear a baby crying. She opened it with the child in her arms, her face bleak.

'Oh,' she said, brightening up, 'it's you. Come in. He's been howling since I came home.'

I followed her into a room and sat down on a floppy divan beside a cot.

'He's a lovely baby,' I said, peering at his distorted, enraged face. 'What's his name?'

'Anthony,' she replied, pacing up and down and shaking him in a futile manner. I wondered how long I should wait for decency's sake. 'I'm glad you came,' she said, just as I was edging off the divan.

'Let me hold him,' I said without meaning to. 'Perhaps a change of arms might do something.'

She passed him over and the child, either in shock or surprise, stopped crying. He was as fat and soft as a pig and smelled of sour milk. He pulled my hair and made a gurgling sound.

'That's marvellous,' said Mai. 'I couldn't do a thing with him.'

I dandled Anthony on my knee while Mai produced weak milky tea and custard creams and breathed warm smiles upon me and chattered about Anthony's weight, teeth and so on. To keep myself awake I concentrated on the painting-by-numbers picture of two flamenco dancers on the wall behind her head.

'Have another biscuit,' she said.

'No thanks. I'm not hungry. Do you mind taking Anthony? I think he's wet me.'

'The little rat-bag.' Mai laughed. 'He does that all the time.'

'You haven't got a drink of something?' I asked when the damp bundle was taken from me.

'Drink? Oh you mean drink. I'm sorry, nothing at all.'

'It doesn't matter,' I said carelessly, 'but I'm afraid I can't stop long. I just happened to be passing.'

'Oh, what a shame. I've been so fed up. I was simply dying for a chat with someone.'

Swallowing a mouthful of the tepid milky tea I said, 'OK, chat away. I'll stop for a half hour.'

'Good. Just a sec until I change Anthony.'

'Change him for what?' I called as she dashed off to leave me with the flamenco dancers.

I sank back on the floppy divan, trying to create in my mind an impression of progress towards some goal, but this eluded me. My life seemed to be a vacuum of desperate nothingness. Surely there must be a reason why I was sitting in a floppy divan in the house of a woman I had nothing in common with, married to a man who was my enemy most of the time, and the mother of children I merely tolerated. And Brendan, yes Brendan. What was he to me? A lover? An ally? Or simply a distraction, with his vivid-blue stare which saw nothing or everything? I must break free, I thought, panicking.

Mai entered. 'I think he'll go to sleep,' she whispered. 'And now'—she sat down beside me, breathing hard with the exhaustion of a long-distance runner—'I can relax.

'So,' she added after a two-minute silence, 'where are you going?'

'Nowhere,' I said.

'I thought you were just passing.'

'I wasn't passing to anywhere in particular. I just wanted to go somewhere, but I don't know where exactly. You see—'

'You poor thing,' said Mai, her face looking nondescript without her make-up, 'I know just how you feel.'

'I don't usually feel like this, but Adam gets on my nerves at times. You know how it is when you live with someone—'

'Don't I just. I lived for six months with someone.'

'What happened?' I felt better now that we were rid of Anthony.

'I told you. He buggered off when I became pregnant.'

'Men are swine,' I said.

'Do you know,' she giggled, 'I quite fancied your Adam.'

'I'm not surprised,' I said with a kindly smile. 'Most women do.'

'Not that I am serious,' she assured me. 'It's like you know when you fancy a film star, it's simply—'

'Fantasy?'

'Yeah, fantasy.' She giggled again. 'Imagine telling someone you fancy their husband!'

'Don't worry.' I winked. 'I'm trying to get rid of him.'

We laughed and joked a lot after that and I began to feel I had benefited from my visit; so much so that I invited her to come to our house the first Saturday she could manage and bring Anthony. When I left she stood on the landing with Anthony in her arms.

'Wave to your Auntie Betty,' she said. He hid his head in her shoulder and howled. On the bus I calculated whether I had enough for a half-bottle of sherry, which I would drink alone in the toilet. It was quite nice to be going back.

CHAPTER SIX

'Handsome is as handsome does,' my mother had said of Adam.

'At least he is handsome,' I had retorted.

'Leave the fellow alone,' said my father. 'She could have done worse.'

'His family were a funny lot,' said my mother. 'His mother's first husband hanged himself.'

'He was no relation to Adam,' I said.

My mother said, 'They say she drove him to it.'

'She didn't manage to drive Adam's old man to it.'

'Well, he was a big man,' said my mother. 'He took a good bucket every Friday, and when he returned from the pub Adam had to wait at the bottom of their stairs so he could help his father up to the door—a wee skinny thing Adam was then. I felt sorry for him.'

'I don't remember that,' I said.

'Well, he was a lot older than you. Besides you weren't allowed near their place—very low-class people in that district.'

'Many's the drink I had with Adam's old man; clever he was, self-educated. Was gassed in the first war. Told me he spent a lot of time reading—said he believed in communism, but not in the party members.'

My mother sniffed. 'Communism indeed. I might have known.'

My father took off his Woolworth's spectacles and shook them at my mother. 'Don't you get uppity over Adam's old man. Many's the letter he wrote to the papers exposing the government for what it was.'

'And I could never understand a word of them,' said my mother.

'I don't know why I bother to come and see you both. You're always arguing.'

'And I suppose you and Adam never argue.'

'Not as much as you two.'

This was true but I didn't mention the heavy sullen silences that had hung on the air like a thick fog in the early days of our marriage. It was only when I began to share the drink with Adam that my tongue was eventually released.

'Anyway,' said my father, 'Adam's old man wrote a fine letter for me when I was sacked from Langton's sausage factory, and we couldn't get a penny from the means test. A fellow called on us after the letter was sent and gave us some money.'

'Ten shillings,' said my mother.

'We would have got bugger all otherwise.'

'I saw Adam's father when he was dying. I don't think he liked me.'

'Christ Almighty,' said my father, 'if you've got cancer I don't expect you like anyone.'

'He was always moody even without cancer,' said my mother. 'And I know for a fact he didn't like me.'

'He thought I'd no character,' I said.

'See what I mean,' said my mother. 'That's what happens when your daughter marries beneath her. They try to bring her down to their level.'

'He was right,' I said. 'I had no character in those days.'

'Ah well,' said my father, 'character's only another name for cheek and you've always had plenty of that.'

I asked my mother for the loan of five bob until I got my wages.

She sniffed. 'I notice you only come round nowadays when you need something.'

'Give her five bob for Christ's sake,' said my father. 'She's your daughter, not some bloody Arab.'

'Or communist,' I added.

87

'So long as it's not for drink,' said my mother, delving into her purse.

'Drink?'

'You've been seen in the licensed grocer's.'

'I don't think our Betty would take to drink when there are kids to be fed,' said my father.

'I was in the licensed grocer's for Adam, not for myself.'

My mother threw her hands in the air. 'See what I mean, he sends her for drink!'

'At least he doesn't booze in the pub,' I said with heat. 'It's not as if the odd bottle of sherry costs that much.'

'Nothing wrong in going to the pub for a pint with the lads,' said my father, lifting up his newspaper. 'Can't stand furtive drinkers, though.'

'If you two are finished with the snide remarks I'll be off—unless you want your money back in case I drink it,' I said to my mother.

'So long as you pay it back, I don't care what you do with it,' she answered. She walked me to the outside door and stood with her arms folded while I shut the gate of their council garden as neat as a giant postage stamp. 'Give my regards to Adam,' she called, possibly for the benefit of the neighbours.

I bought some sherry with the five shillings. It wasn't much, only a half-bottle, but it might

88

placate Adam, who hadn't been speaking to me
recently.

'Taking to drink, are you?' he asked.

'If you can't beat them, join them.'

I saluted his glass with the greatest of aplomb
and after one drink became flushed and garru-
lous, interrupting him when he started on the
inevitable topic of his army days.

'What about that one you met in Italy?'
I asked.

'What one?'

'The Christina one.'

'What's brought this on?'

'I just remembered how you spoke about her
before we were married. I haven't heard much
about her since.'

'Did I? What did I say?'

'You apparently had a big thing going with
her. You said something about helping her
to climb a gate and putting your hand up
her skirt.'

Adam groaned. 'If I had known I was going
to be lumbered with you I would have kept my
big mouth shut.'

'Well, you didn't—so tell me about her
again.'

'There's nothing more to add. Over the
fence, onto the grass, and then what every
man does.'

'I want you to go into detail.'

89

'Is this what gives you a kick?'

I laid down my empty glass and pushed myself onto his knee. 'I don't know. Tell me so that I can find out.'

I stroked his hair and kissed his eyes while he went into the graphic details.

'You're a dirty bastard,' I said when he stopped talking.

'I made it up to please you.'

'No you didn't.' I punched his chest with my fists.

'God's sake, kid, what do you expect? It was before I met you. It was the war.'

'It's always the war.' I was crying, but something inside me was enjoying it.

'I love you—only you,' he said. 'Come to bed and I'll prove it.'

So I did.

*

Life's full of surprises. Tonight Brendan did not come. We set off for the pub, if not arm-in-arm at least companionable, but we are always companionable at this stage. Half an hour passed as we sat toying with beer and waiting for Brendan. We felt it unfair to start guzzling before he arrived—besides he always bought the first round. We mentioned the heat, the flat beer, the weather, then gave up. The study of human behaviour in animals came to

my mind, a promising subject, but dangerous.
I let it pass.

'What the hell's keeping him?' said Adam.

'He's not obliged to come,' I pointed out.

'It's not like him.'

'He could have something else to do.'

'Brendan doing something else? He'd be lost
without us.'

'It's not normal though. He's not even in
our age group and he clings to us as if he
was our son. Wonder what he does for sex,'
I said reflectively.

'What any man does when he has to go
without.' I sensed bitterness in Adam's voice.

'Perhaps his mother is ill,' I said.

'Perhaps.' Adam approached the bar and
returned with two short drinks. I scowled at
the glass he placed before me.

'What's wrong? Don't you want this?'

'We should have stayed at home.' The image
of home increased my depression.

'I thought you liked getting away from home,'
said Adam, staring at me like a hawk. His face
looked gaunt and the old acne marks from
adolescence made him look like a smallpox
victim. Perhaps it was the angle of the fluor-
escent lighting.

'You never know what the kids will be up
to,' I said.

'We'll go home then.'

I narrowed my eyes and looked around at all the well-occupied tables.

'Pubs are lonely places,' I declared.

'Lonely—Jesus, what next?'

'You can't say they are friendly. No one ever speaks to us—except Brendan.'

'People are just minding their own business,' said Adam.

'Why bother to drink to mind their own business?' I smiled wildly at a woman at the table opposite who had caught my eye. Her lips creased slightly before she turned to her companion.

'OK, let's go,' said Adam. He swallowed his drink, stood up and marched outwards. I paused for a second, but aware of the ignominy of appearing discarded I rushed after him.

When we opened our backdoor Brendan was standing in the kitchenette with his back against the wall. The kids sat on the kitchen chairs studying him as if he was on show. We also studied him. There was something wrong.

'Look at Brendan's trousers,' said Robert, pointing.

We looked. One trouser bottom was torn and his exposed ankle looked bloody.

'Your good suit?' I said.

'Been in a fight?' asked Adam.

'It's ruined,' said Brendan, 'and I haven't even made the first payment.'

I said, 'Perhaps it could be sewn. What happened?'

'A fucking dog. A vicious rat of a thing that came out from nowhere and pounced on me. Then it bit my ankles before I could as much as turn. Look at that!'

We both looked.

'It's not the end of the world,' Adam said jocularly, eyeing the bottle Brendan had placed on the table.

'Your ankle is in some mess with all that blood,' I said. Brendan smiled as he surveyed his ankle. I was glad to see him cheer up.

'That's not my blood,' he said. 'It's the dog's. I kicked its head in and threw it over the hedge. It's dead.'

Adam and I regarded each other, slightly open-mouthed.

'You rotten pig,' said Rae, her face all crumpled.

'Don't be a stupid bitch,' said Robert to his sister. 'It was a big dog. It attacked Brendan.'

'Was it an Alsatian?' Adam asked.

Brendan thought for a minute. 'It wasn't an Alsatian, it was one of those small, white, furry dogs.' His forehead puckered. 'What do you call them again?'

'A poodle,' I suggested.

'Perhaps,' he said, examining again his trouser bottom.

Adam opened the bottle and poured out three glasses. I looked at Brendan's torn trousers with his podgy white legs showing and shuddered.

'Perhaps you could sew it up,' said Brendan, 'so that my mother won't notice it. She's going to be real mad.' He gave me one of his vivid-blue stares.

'Sew it yourself,' I said, expecting Adam to butt in and tell me off, but he didn't.

He said, 'Don't you think you went a bit far, killing the animal? I can understand a kick, but—'

'It ruined my suit,' said Brendan firmly.

'I don't like you any more. You're cruel to animals,' said Rae.

'It's not that when you're throwing stones at the cat next door,' I told her.

'But we've never killed it,' said Robert. 'We always aim to miss.'

Rae went into the cupboard and brought out a bottle two inches full of milk. 'I'm going to feed that cat, and you'—she pointed to Brendan—'had better not kill it.'

'That's all the milk we've got,' I began, but she had gone out the door with Robert following.

Brendan looked sad. 'They don't understand.'

'Neither do we,' said Adam.

'Let's forget it,' I said. Then I told Brendan I would sew his trousers later on.

Brendan beamed. 'Thanks, Betty. You're a pal.'

Adam said reflectively, 'You must have put the boot in real hard to kill it.'

I said, 'It wasn't that when you shot down a German pilot baling out of his plane. You killed a man. That was worse.'

'That was different,' said Adam. 'It was the war. We didn't know what we were doing half the time.'

'Yeah,' I sneered. 'There is still a good difference between a man and a dog.' But it took another two drinks for me to look Brendan full in the face.

When eventually I did I told him to go and wash his ankle in the bathroom, but that I was sorry I just remembered I had no thread. He shuffled off limping.

'What a state to get into,' said Adam.

'Killing a dog like that gives me the creeps.'

'Probably lost the head.'

'It's obvious he lost the head, but it still gives me the creeps.'

'Have you any iodine?' Adam asked.

'No, we don't,' I snapped.

'I'm sure we had some thread.'

'I'm damned if I'm going to touch his trousers, stiff with some animal's gore. Anyway

I can't be bothered. Between one thing and another it's been a rotten night.'

'It doesn't give you the creeps to take his drink.'

'If I have to put up with you and him I'm due to take his drink.' Defiantly I poured myself out a glassful.

'Steady on,' said Adam. I handed him the bottle and he poured himself one with the look of a person who is merely being obliging. 'Anyway,' he added, 'if a guy loses his head once in a blue moon he's entitled to. He doesn't have much of a life at the best of times.'

'Who has, but we don't go around kicking dogs to death.'

Brendan came into the room at that moment.

'OK now?' asked Adam.

He held out his foot. There was nothing to see. He had pinned the torn cloth together. 'Nips a bit—hope it isn't poisoned.'

'I'm trying to forget all about your ankle,' I said in a cold voice, 'so let's drop the subject.'

'She's in a bad mood,' said Adam. 'Probably her time in the month.'

Brendan looked at me puzzled.

'Here, take a drink,' I said to him to avoid any more complications.

'You're not still angry with me?' Brendan asked, some time later, when Adam had gone to the toilet. Then he did a strange thing. He went down on one knee and kissed my hand. 'Please forgive me,' he said. 'I can't stand you being angry with me.'

I kissed the top of his head. His hair was thick and greasy, unlike Adam's fine growth. 'Of course I'm not angry with you any more.' How could I be angry with Brendan in such a position of worship?

'I see you two have made it up,' said Adam, entering. His voice was finely sarcastic. Brendan got to his feet clumsily. I tapped my head at Adam to indicate I was humouring an idiot.

*

On Sunday afternoon I sat in Mr Robson's study, looking around and faintly surprised, but then Mr Robson is a surprising man. The walls of his study were decorated everywhere with photographs. Some of them were framed and some were only snapshots pinned on. At a quick guess there must have been around two hundred of them.

'Memories,' he said.

'Is your wife. .?' I felt duty bound to ask.

He pointed to one of the larger framed ones. The features were indistinct like an early silent movie—smudged eyes and bushy hair.

'She was a lovely woman,' I said.

'Not really,' he said. 'She was quite plain in fact.' His finger moved quickly away from his wife and stabbed the print of a young man with a steadfast gaze.

'Your son?'

'I have no family. This face is not one I wish to see in my dreams, but I feel obliged to record his memory. He was hanged, you see.'

'Hanged,' I repeated.

'It was a long time ago. I was his lawyer, one of my early cases, but my engagement was only a formality. The evidence against him was too damaging. He had cut the throats of his parents and his young sister while they were asleep. I tried for insanity, but since he was so obviously intelligent it did not come off.' Mr Robson sighed. 'I rather liked him. As I said he was very intelligent, and it was not often I had to deal with intelligent people.'

'But what he did was horrible.'

'I agree, but it's unreasonable to expect everyone to be reasonable or rational. Now and then the mind keels over from some apparently trivial cause. It could be compared to the sudden emergence of a pimple on the face. One doesn't want the pimple, but there it is.'

'Perhaps he had a pimple on the brain,' I said with a feeble stab at humour.

'Who knows, my dear—that is a very good comparison; but in his case the pimple vanished as quickly as it came, leaving no evidence of a disturbed mind—which was unfortunate for him.'

We stood for a moment deliberating on the steadfast gaze of the hanged man, then Mr Robson took off his spectacles and wiped them assiduously with a small piece of yellow cloth, saying, 'Before we start I wonder if you would be so kind as to partake of a cup of herbal tea with me. It tastes quite excellent and is beneficial to the health.'

I said that I'd love to, mainly because I wanted to escape from the photographs.

'We'll take it in my kitchen. It's much cosier.'

The kitchen was brightly tiled and a wonder of gleaming equipment. I could happily have spent my life in that shining order. With neat, precise movements he placed two cups and saucers, probably china ones, on a polished kitchen table beside the window. The tea, which had evidently been prepared beforehand, was poured from a silver tea-pot, and two plain digestive biscuits were produced to enhance the ceremony. I wasn't keen on the herbal tea but said it was very nice when he asked me what I thought.

'Some people have to acquire the taste,' he explained. 'Like music, poetry, painting and all works of art.'

I thought he was going on a bit about what

was only a cup of tea, after all. 'I understand what you mean,' I said. 'I never used to appreciate Beethoven, but after I listened to him once or twice I enjoyed it immensely.' This statement was fabrication as I never listen to any kind of classical music if I can help it. I changed the subject quickly lest he began to discuss Beethoven. 'You have a lovely house.'

'It's modest, but peaceful,' he admitted.

I reflected on our house with its tatty, stained furniture and frayed carpets. 'Yes, it's very peaceful.' Hastily I swallowed the last of my herbal tea and regarded him expectantly for the next course of action, but his eyes were straying out the window.

'It was different when my wife was alive. Flowery and frilly, it was. I've had it refurnished to my taste.'

'I see. I suppose,' I said, 'you will miss her?'

'Who? Oh you mean my wife. Yes, I suppose I did, at the time. Now I'm quite happy to be alone. It lets me do what I want. Not,' he said with a wink, 'that I do very much, at my age.'

I tittered uneasily. 'Still it's nice that you are—'

'Yes, isn't it?' He now sounded bored with the subject. 'Shall we retire to the study?'

I jumped up, glad to be moving, but feeling more uneasy with Mr Robson in his house than I did at the office, which was probably because of the strange surroundings. He gave me pages of meaningless data to type, or if not quite meaningless, extremely boring, and rather like a social worker's study of various clients; but as it was a study on social behaviour it was bound to be like that. I had typed three reports on individuals named John, Timothy and Maurice. I paused at a bit where it stated Maurice had sexual aberrations which were similar to those discovered in white mice after injections of hormones. 'Sounds fun,' I said aloud, and wondered how much I would get paid for all this bumf. Lunch was another formal affair in the kitchen with Mr Robson. The chicken salad and boiled beetroot were enjoyable, but sharing it with him gave me claustrophobia.

'Would you care to see my garden?' he asked. He looked eager and timid at the same time.

'I'd love to,' I said, glad to get out in the fresh air. Making appropriate appreciative noises I looked at the neat flowering borders.

'I've just been thinking,' he said, tapping me on the shoulder, 'that you would make a delightful study for one of the chapters in my book.'

'I would?' I stepped back in surprise, the heel of my shoe sinking into the earth. 'Oh dear,' I said, looking at the hole I had made.

'Don't worry. The gardener will soon sort that out.'

'You have a gardener?'

'Yes, but he's been off for three weeks with a bad back, an affliction common to gardeners. I expect him to return next week. He only comes for a couple of days anyway.'

'A gardener,' I said. 'I wonder if—'

'Don't worry about the garden,' he said impatiently. 'Now, as I was saying, I think you would make a delightful study—'

'Yes, Mr Robson, I know what you said, but what does that mean exactly?'

'It's really quite painless.' He laughed waggishly. 'I ask certain simple questions and you give me certain simple answers from which I draw certain conclusions.'

The words 'sexual aberrations' hung on my mind. 'Would I have to take drugs or injections?'

He laughed heartily. 'My dear, I am not exactly Dr Frankenstein. Of course not. The questions would be less than embarrassing, but sometimes with female conclusions I am often working in the dark, so to speak, and any data I have gained in the past from the female species was never conclusive enough, for reasons I will not go into. So what do you say? I will pay you adequately, if not handsomely.'

'I will have to consider this, Mr Robson, if you don't mind.'

'Naturally, my dear. Take your time. At the moment I'm happy enough with the typing.'

Before we turned into the house I said, 'By the way, I can get you a gardener if you are stuck for one.' Before Mr Robson could open his mouth I said quickly, 'He's very dependable and strong and very good at his job and he doesn't charge all that much.' I had no idea what Brendan charged.

Mr Robson said, 'Well, this fellow that usually comes—'

'It would only be until he came back.'

Mr Robson looked at me quizzically. 'This gardener wouldn't be your friend Brendan by any chance?'

'It is.' I made my eyes wide and candid.

'I see.' He walked ahead of me into the study slightly hen-toed. I noticed, being taller than him, that though his scalp shone through his thin hair he sported a double crown. I also have a double crown, which my mother always maintained was unlucky. I sat down at the desk with its pile of papers. Mr Robson peered at the papers I had typed.

'You are getting along nicely,' he said.

'It's interesting work.'

'Do you find the subjects interesting?' he asked eagerly.

'Totally absorbing,' I said. 'In fact,' I added, 'the part about Maurice—the one with the

103

sexual aberrations—was fascinating, although I wished I had more time to go into it deeply.'

'Did you really?' said Mr Robson. He bestowed on me an approving glance as if he had discovered a talented pupil. 'Why were you fascinated?'

'I don't know really.' I paused, then continued, 'I believe Brendan has sexual aberrations.'

Mr Robson pondered, then stated, 'From what you said about him I'm not surprised, but then,' he patted me on the shoulder, 'most of us have.'

'Perhaps,' I said, moving about to dislodge his warm old hand. 'Though some may have more than others.'

'Tell him to call on me any time after six o'clock,' said Mr Robson. 'The weeds are getting out of hand.'

I thanked him, then told him there was something else on my mind that was rather disturbing as well as embarrassing.

'Spit it out, my dear. You need not be embarrassed with me.'

'The women in the office are beginning to talk.'

'Talk? You mean talk about us?'

'Well,' I said, blinking my eyes, 'it's one of them in particular. She's trying to make something out of me coming here to type for you.'

Mr Robson's small eyes twinkled. 'An old man like me and an attractive young woman, that is flattering.' To my annoyance he ruffled my hair.

'Nevertheless, it's very upsetting.'

'Who is the woman who is causing the talk?'

'The one called Mai, with the black hair and painted face.'

'That one! Yes, well, I could never take to her—looks like a streetwalker to me.'

'Perhaps she would make a good study,' I said mischievously.

'No depth to her. She'd be no use to study. Besides, I wouldn't trust her the way I trust you.'

'She's not a bad person really,' I said. 'She likes to create situations.'

'A troublemaker, in other words,' he said sternly. 'We can't have that.'

'You won't get rid of her,' I said anxiously. 'She has a baby you know, and—'

'An unmarried mother!' said Mr Robson in a scandalised way.

'Please don't let on I told you that. I'm really sorry for her.'

'You are simply too sensitive, my dear.'

He left the room and I typed on for another two hours. After that he called me up to his bedroom, which was a simple affair, containing

105

a double bed covered with a heavy brocade bedmat, a small set of drawers and a large screen. He stroked my hair, my face and my breasts for some minutes, then retired behind the screen. I sat on the edge of the bed hearing small panting noises, then a low painful groan, but as I wasn't involved in this I considered I had been let off lightly.

He emerged from the screen quite composed and asked me if I could manage the following Sunday, handing me a ten-pound note.

'Certainly, Mr Robson,' I said. 'And what about Brendan?'

'Yes, by all means,' he said.

*

At lunch-time there was no sign of Mai anywhere. I was neither surprised nor curious about that. Good riddance, I thought. I would go and see Mrs Rossi instead. Who knows, she might be in the mood to read my cards.

'Sit down,' she said. I thought she looked surly, but I was encouraged by Poppy's friendly glance as she brought in the silver tray with all its accessories, including biscuits, though actually I longed for a sandwich.

'That will be all, dear,' said Mrs Rossi.

Poppy winked at me before she left. I would have liked to wink back but Mrs Rossi was watching me.

106

'Impudent bitch,' she said when the door banged shut.

'Why do you employ her then?' I asked.

'She's my niece. I like to keep things in the family. Is there something in particular you want to see me about?'

'I was wondering if you could read my cards to find out if there's anything good happening in the future. I feel as though I'm going through a dark patch.'

She looked at me closely and said, 'I notice you've got a widow's peak.'

'Is that significant?' I asked.

'Could be.'

'But why do you think it's significant?'

'My, you're a one for the questions.' She placed her forefinger on her lip and closed her eyes. The effect was very impressive. She opened her eyes suddenly, catching my fascination with her solitaire diamond ring. 'More often than you would think,' she added.

'I wouldn't want anything to happen to my husband,' I said.

'Of course not, but whatever is going to happen will happen.'

I could see she wasn't going to bring out the cards. I thought I'd change the subject.

'Mr Robson has two crowns. Is this unlucky?'

'It depends.' She added with a cautious glance, 'Is he still as weird?'

'Not all that much.'

'Self-centred then?'

'Maybe. Do you know him well?'

'Well enough. He once asked Poppy round to his house to do some typing.'

I kept my voice flat. 'Did she go?'

'Not that I know of, though you never know with her. She keeps a lot to herself.'

'Does she?' I said, thinking of Poppy's con-spiratorial wink.

'Besides,' Mrs Rossi added, 'she can't type for nuts. I don't know why I keep her on, family or not.'

She brought the cards out from a drawer under her desk and asked if I wanted a quick gaze at the future.

'Oh yes,' I said. 'That's why I came.'

The cards were dealt. Mrs Rossi gave a long serious glance at each of them in turn while I sat holding my breath.

'What do you see?' I asked, unable to stand the tension.

She waved my question aside as though it was interfering with her concentration. She dealt another one and said, 'This is interesting.'

'What is?' I asked.

She meditated on the card for a while, then confronted me with eyes glowing like hot tar. 'You'd better watch your step.'

'Why?'

'I don't know; there's a kind of black shadow here. I can't be specific.'

'If you can't be specific how can I be careful? I can't shut myself up in a room all day.'

'Don't get angry,' she said. 'When it comes to it you will know what to beware of. Just a warning, my dear.'

I wanted to tell her I didn't believe that she saw anything in the cards, and was simply making it up, but wisely I said nothing.

*

In the afternoon, when I was sitting at my desk in the office stuffing myself with a roll and cheese purchased from a snack van, Mai came over and asked me to come out to the toilet.

'What for?' I asked with a show of resentment, though inwardly I felt apprehensive and guilty.

'Just come,' she said. 'I can't talk here.' This was reasonable enough. Faces were beginning to turn in our direction.

In the toilet she was wiping off the mascara from her smudged eyes. Without the black stuff they looked surprisingly small. 'I've been sacked,' she said.

'You've been what?' I wished she would put the mascara back on. She looked vulnerable without it.

'Didn't you notice I was in Mr Robson's

room for a full hour?' Her eyes brimmed with tears.

'I wasn't paying any attention. I thought you had gone home. Why has he sacked you? He's not your boss anyway.'

'I know he isn't,' she burst out peevishly, 'but he seems to have the power to sack people.'

'But why?'

'He said it had been brought to his attention that my work has been careless of late.' Her shoulders heaved with short sobs. 'It hasn't been any worse than usual.'

'That's rotten,' I said, 'but you shouldn't worry about it. This place is a dumping ground for old women anyway. You'll get another job easily.'

'It's the disgrace of it.'

'Why didn't you see your own boss?'

'That old bitch Benson? I did, and she said my time-keeping was bad. It's no worse than anyone else's. Yours is much worse come to think of it.'

'Come now, Mai, it's not my fault,' I said.

'Someone's got it in for me anyway.'

'Are you sure you didn't tell anyone else about your baby? You know how they are in here.'

'Only you.' She was reapplying the mascara. Now she looked more like her old self.

'I didn't say anything,' I said. 'Anyway, I'm

thinking of chucking it myself. Old Robson's getting on my nerves. I think you're lucky in a way, being forced to move on. Wouldn't it be great to work for someone handsome and sexy?'

'You're right,' said Mai, brightening at the mention of sex. 'This place is a dead end. When do you think you'll leave?'

'I'll give it another week. The agency hasn't got anything to offer right now. I've already asked them.'

'Perhaps I should try your agency.'

'I suppose you could,' I said doubtfully. 'So long as you're prepared to wait. Mrs Rossi is always fully booked up.'

'Pity,' said Mai, gathering her make-up spread before her like a theatrical kit. She smoothed down her skirt and looked at the back of her legs to make sure her stocking seams were straight, then she squared her shoulders and sighed.

'I might as well go now. At least I've got two weeks' wages to blow—that is if I get another job at once.'

'I'm sorry to see you leave,' I said, truly regretful.

'I'll phone you as soon as I get something and we can meet again for lunch.'

'Oh God,' I groaned. 'I'll have no one to talk to over lunch now.'

She squeezed my hand in sympathy. 'Don't worry, I'll get in touch.'

She whisked out of the toilet leaving me vaguely depressed. I hadn't thought she would get the sack, only a reprimand, perhaps, for spreading gossip. Mr Robson had certainly taken my point. What was I getting into anyway with the old goat? But when I thought about it there wasn't much I could do except to play the cards dealt me as well as I could.

CHAPTER SEVEN

A dam and I had not been on speaking terms, apart from uttering the barest requests like, 'Pass the salt,' or, 'What's for eating?' The funereal atmosphere even affected the kids, who crept around like orphans in the custody of a hostile foster-parent. A bottle of wine would have remedied the silence but it went against the grain to make any overtures. It was boring to sit at the open window after the dreary business of eating, watching Adam dig the garden with the air of a martyr, but boredom has always enveloped my life like a continually recurring cloud. I heard Robert rummaging in the kitchen cupboard.

'What are you looking for?' I shouted.

'Daddy says I've to get a trowel to dig up the weeds.'

'There is no such thing in this house.'

'Well Daddy says—'

'Pull them out with your hands.'

The rummaging continued with a lot of noise. I joined Robert crouched in the cupboard, looking through an assortment of items which would have depressed a rag-and-bone merchant.

'I have told you—' I began, and broke off. Robert had dislodged what appeared to be an old, empty wine bottle, but I had the feeling it wasn't empty. I pulled it out. It was three-quarters full. The cloud lifted immediately. 'Tell Daddy there is no trowel,' I said gently. 'Tomorrow I'll buy one.'

'Tomorrow is no use,' Robert said bitterly, backing out of the cupboard.

After a glass of the wine I was in a brighter mood. 'Adam,' I called out of the window, displaying the bottle. At first he looked insulted and continued to dig. Five minutes later he entered.

'What?'

'Look what I've found,' I said, handing him a glass.

'You found it?'

'Among the junk in the cupboard when Robert was looking for a trowel.'

Adam wiped his hands on his trousers, saying it was an ill wind et cetera. We sat down in the warmth coming from the open window, sipping the wine with dainty appreciation. I

114

drew marks on the dusty table. 'At least we are speaking,' I said.

'Are we?' His face was friendly.

'You know there is no harm in my typing for Mr Robson. After all I did get five pounds.'

'I suppose not,' he admitted. 'What did you do with the fiver anyway?' he added. 'I never saw much sign of it.'

'I'm saving up.'

'You are?'

'It's not for myself. I thought we might go for a holiday, somewhere near the sea. The kids would love that, wouldn't they?'

'Suppose so,' he said slowly, 'but how many more fivers do you have to earn to accomplish that?'

'I can only do my best. At least it's a start.'

'I'll say this much for you, kid'—he caught my wrist as it reached out for the bottle—'you're a trier. You deserve something better than me.'

I laughed. 'I know, but at the moment I've only got you.'

When the bottle was finished I purchased another. We sat in the garden on a blanket with the bottle and the glasses. The kids ran around chasing the cat next door with Adam's spade. The man next door viewed us over the hedge. We waved at him. He turned away sullenly.

Adam said, 'This is the life.'

'Just like the poem,' I said.

'Of course. A loaf of bread, a flask of wine and thou—'

'Beside me singing in the wilderness,' I added. I looked at Adam affectionately. I would really miss him if he went out of my life, but some day he would have to go.

*

When I was very young, before the war, I took it for granted that if my parents were not exactly rich they were not poor; that is, poor in the sense that you didn't get twopence for the Saturday matinée, a penny for sweets, and a penny for a comic. The fact that the comic cost twopence and I always had to steal the extra penny from my mother was nothing to do with being poor, since she never missed it—sometimes not even missing as much as twopence.

'Now don't get the sausages at fourpence a pound or the ones at eightpence, get the ones at sixpence,' she would instruct me. I would get the ones at fourpence, and that was a penny straight away from half a pound of sausages. I loved when I had to go for sausages, but to be sent for threepence worth of mixed vegetables gave me no room for manoeuvre, unless I arrived home tearfully

116

explaining I had dropped a halfpenny down a drain. Another thing that proved we weren't poor was the fact that I had cornflakes for breakfast. My friend across the street had never heard of them. It was when I was sent to the Secondary Academy, a twenty-minute bus journey out of town, that I discovered we were poor. I didn't wear the appropriate clothes with the appropriate school colours, and worse still I had to borrow a hockey stick from the school pavilion when we played the ghastly game.

'Hockey stick!' my mother said in a scandalised voice. 'I'm damned if I'm going to buy a hockey stick when you can borrow one from the school.'

'Everyone else has their own hockey stick.'

'That's too bloody bad.'

On the subject of school colours she relented by knitting me a jumper with a blue and grey collar and waist band. A month later the colours were changed to red and yellow. It was out of the question to tell my mother this, so I retreated into a shell for the three years I attended Morton Academy, and waited at the bus stop yards apart from the giggling girls in red and gold blazers. I once told another unpopular girl with buck teeth and woollen stockings that if she hung about with me I would give her sixpence every week. 'Sez you,' she said, and wandered off with an unholy smile on her face.

Once when we were reminiscing about our childhood I told Adam all this.

'Serves you right for being at that bloody snobbish place.'

'My mother sent me because I was clever.'

'Clever—Jesus, what's that got to do with it? You were a lot better off than me. My old man was always drunk out of his skull.'

'So I heard,' I said coldly.

'At least he knew what life was about.'

'Getting drunk?'

'You've got to get through it the best way you can.'

'That's what I intend to do.'

'I don't know where you get your big ideas from unless it's from your mother.'

'Look, Adam,' I shouted, 'just because I'd like things to be nice—just because I'd like to dress nice and have a nice house—just because I'd like you to be different from your father—'

'My father was his own man. I wish I was like him.'

'You are like him. Is that why you drink so much?'

He hadn't answered, but I remember saying, 'Of course, I forget—it was the war. That's what made you drink.'

He continued to say nothing. I don't mind his drinking now since it's about the only thing we have in common, apart from Brendan and the kids. But I'd still like things to be nice. Mr Robson's house is exceptionally nice.

*

When Brendan appeared on the scene on Friday night as usual I told him I could get him started at the gardening. He didn't look enthusiastic.

'It's extra money,' I pointed out. 'It will help to pay for your suit. I notice you haven't got it on. Didn't your mother sew the trousers?'

'I chucked it in a cupboard. Can't be bothered with it any more.' He added listlessly, 'I prefer my old rags—don't feel right in a suit.'

'That's not the point, old man,' said Adam. 'You've still got to pay for it.'

'Not unless,' I said, 'he expects his mother to pay for it.'

Adam looked at me balefully, then asked Brendan, 'How's the ankle—healed up?'

'It was only a scratch,' said Brendan, shifting from one leg to another, with hands in his pockets.

'Poor dog,' I said.

'No sense bringing the dog up,' said Adam. 'It's long gone.'

'But it's so irritating,' I said. 'To think a dog has been kicked to death because it tore

119

Brendan's trousers, which he's chucked in a cupboard, and his mother will have to pay for them when he could have a job and at least pay for them himself and have a bit extra to spend at the same time.'

Adam laughed. 'That's like the old woman who swallowed a fly.'

'I'll think about the job,' said Brendan. 'Are you two coming out to the pub?'

'Supposing I said no,' I said.

'That's fine. Brendan and me will go ourselves.'

'We can't leave Betty,' said Brendan, giving me one of his vivid-blue stares.

'Who can't?' said Adam. 'She'll only nark at you all night about this job. You know it's for the same old guy she types for, not only at the office mark you. She goes to his house to type.' He uttered this in a significant way to Brendan.

'I didn't know that,' said Brendan, as if I had been keeping secrets from him.

'Mr Robson is a very nice old man. I put in a good word for you about doing his garden—thought you would be pleased.'

'But I am pleased. It was good of you. You're right—I could pay up the suit easily. Maybe I could get something else out of the catalogue—something that would suit me better, ha ha.'

'You're some guy,' said Adam, smiling and shaking his head.

'Well I hope that's settled then so that I can tell Mr Robson you'll start on Monday evening after six.'

'Will you be there?' asked Brendan.

'No, but don't worry. I'll tell him you're a good worker.'

'What about getting me a job at the gardening?' asked Adam.

My eyes widened. 'I didn't think you would take it, but if you like—'

'Forget it,' said Adam. 'He's not going to want two gardeners.'

'I wish you had said—' I began.

'Let's go,' said Adam. 'I'm fed up with all this yacking about gardeners and so on. Are you ready, Brendan?'

He walked out while I was searching for the new handbag bought with some of Mr Robson's money. 'Wait for me,' I called, running after them. Brendan was looking round anxiously like a dog that is torn between two owners.

*

Lunch-time was lonesome without Mai. I almost choked over my food in the hurry to get away from the diners around me. Not many people, it appeared, eat alone. Outside in the clammy drizzle of a summer day it was less claustrophobic, though shop windows taunted me with displays of garments I couldn't afford. I walked through Woolworth's and managed to sneak a manicure set into my bag. I was filing my nails in the office cloakroom when Miss Benson entered tutting about the rain. Then she said, 'Aren't you early?'

'Just one of those days when you're glad to get back inside.'

'Perhaps you're missing your friend?' she said, her eyes as bright and as knowing as a squirrel's.

'I think it was a rotten thing to happen.'

'What was?' She shook the rain from her plastic coat fussily.

'To get her books like that. She thinks some-one had it in for her.'

'Well, it wasn't me,' she said, her voice unnecessarily shrill.

'I never thought it was you. I've always considered you a fair-minded person.'

'I am,' she said in a grateful tone. 'I've never known anyone to leave so quickly. I'm not sure what happened. Do you?'

I sighed. 'Not really, but it just goes to show.'

'Show what?'

'That no one's safe here. I'm glad I'm only temporary.'

'I've been here for twenty years, and I've

always been treated with the greatest consideration. If you do your work well there is no question of your position being unsafe.'

I shrugged. 'I'm sure you know this firm better than I do. Twenty years is a long time.'

'I think we'd better get back to the office,' she said in a fractious tone as she studied her watch.

I stood in the cloakroom for another two minutes after she'd gone. I wasn't going to do what she told me. I was independent, after all.

*

Later I sat in Mr Robson's room, waiting while he checked the letters I had typed in the morning. He nodded while peering along the words like a hen pecking on gravel. I considered he was being unnecessarily particular. Usually he simply signed the letters after a brief glance.

'Everything all right?' I asked.

'One or two small errors.' His face creased into a reproving smile. 'And look, there is a smudge at the top of this one.' He pulled out the offending letter.

'I see,' I said, staring at his pointing finger.

'Nothing to worry about, my dear.' He coughed apologetically.

I stared into his face, which reminded me of a tortoise with all its creases. 'Perhaps it was thinking about Sunday that made me careless.'

123

'Sunday,' he repeated, frowning, as though he could not recall anything about it.

'Yes, Sunday,' I said, with a darkening suspicion he might be suffering from amnesia. 'You remember Sunday?'

'Certainly I remember Sunday.' He drew his chair close in to the table, his knees touching mine. 'You did very well on Sunday and I trust this Sunday you will do equally well.' He coughed again saying, 'But if you would just take out this smudge with your rubber I would be very much obliged.'

'What about the other small errors?'

'There's nothing much. I'll let them pass.'

'If I'm to stay on permanently—' I began.

'Yes?' he said, fixing me with his rheumy eyes.

'I only said if, but if I do stay on permanently do I get any more money?' I asked this gently so as not to startle him.

'Certainly, you will get a little more money. Anyone who pleases me is always rewarded.'

'I don't suppose I would get as much as Miss Benson, since she has been here for twenty years.'

'Miss Benson,' he said with a wink, 'has never pleased me at all.'

Before I left I told him that Brendan had promised to come and dig his garden.

*

'Teacher says you've to give me money for wool,' said Rae. We were having pies and beans for the meal, which was popular with the kids, but not with Adam. I had run out of ideas.

'Wool,' I repeated, trying to cut the hard, burnt crust of the pie.

'Take it in your hands,' said Adam, 'like a chop, which I have dim memories of eating long ago.'

'Yeah, and teacher says the collar of my shirt is dirty,' said Robert.

'Christ's sake,' I said. 'Who does teacher think she is?'

'My teacher is a man.'

'He must be an old poof if he notices your collar.'

'What's a poof?' asked Rae.

'Something you sit on,' said Robert.

I had to laugh, but Adam was frozen-faced. 'That's right, something like your father.'

'Are you going to start?' I demanded, pushing aside the pie.

'With all the money you earn, I expect something better than this.'

'Do you now?' I shook with loathing for him. 'So this is what it's all about? What the hell do you expect with all the boozing you do?'

'And you,' he said.

'And who pays for it?' I had a terrible urge

to throw my plate against the wall, but I would only have to clean up the mess.

'Tell you what I'll do,' said Adam, standing up and pushing back his chair. 'I'm going to see someone.'

'A man about a dog,' I sneered.

'No, a man about a job.' He picked up his jacket draped over the chair and slammed out.

'See what you've done,' I blasted the kids, 'talking about wool and dirty collars. Now you've given him the excuse.'

Rae started to whine.

'Shut up you,' said Robert.

'Who are you telling to shut up?' I said to him.

'You're always nagging,' snarled Robert and ran out of the room.

If only I could pack up and leave it all I thought, but I had no suitcase, no clothes and, worst of all, no money. I must save up, not for a holiday, but for a change of address. I could send for the kids after it was all fixed. Adam could do what he liked. Our marriage was a ghastly mistake, always had been. No use expecting miracles to happen. He wasn't going to vanish. Meantime I must wash the dishes and tidy up a bit before I could do anything.

'Stop crying,' I told Rae. 'I'll get your wool tomorrow.'

126

'Where's Daddy gone?' she said, her snivelling dying down to sniffs.

'You heard him. For a job, so he says.'

'He's not leaving us, is he?'

'I shouldn't think so. Go and play. I've got things to do.'

I washed the dishes, then located one of Robert's shirts and scrubbed the collar while my mind was afire with plans that faded as soon as they formed. Finally I sank into a chair worn out by the contention inside my head. 'I know I've plenty of faults,' I told myself, 'but I do think I've tried my best to be a good wife and mother, and while I understand I shouldn't drink so much, the fact is if I didn't drink when Adam drinks I would go out of my mind. As for Mr Robson, I have done nothing to be ashamed of, nothing that anyone can prove anyway, and as for Brendan, if I've done anything to be ashamed of it was more out of pity than anything else. Surely it is only fair that I leave all this confusion for a better life. After all, we're only here for a few fleeting moments, as Adam often says. Why not make the best of them?' My mind swivelled back to the question, where was the bastard and what was he doing. What right had he to do anything? I was the victim, not him. I went outside to look for the kids but they had vanished. Walking along the street I saw them leaning on the fence with some other kids. They seemed happy. I was glad. I could leave them any time. Turning the corner I met Adam.

'Where are you going, kid?' he asked. He looked concerned.

'Anywhere away from you.'

'I've a present for you.' He shoved something into my hand. It was a five-pound note. 'It's all right,' he said as I stared at the money. 'I sold the gold watch.'

'It was your dad's. You'd no right to—'

'Are you coming for a drink?'

'You sold your father's watch for a drink?'

'We'll do something else if you want. I'll buy you something—'

'Don't bother.'

We were walking along the street. 'What do you want?' he asked, breaking the silence.

'Nothing really.'

We entered the pub and ordered two drinks.

'You shouldn't have done it,' I said.

'What use was the watch to anyone? It was no use to my father.'

'It had sentimental value.'

He laughed. 'To you—not to me. A watch means nothing. I can remember my old man without a watch.'

'I suppose so.' I sipped the whisky carefully.

'Drink up. I'll get another, not unless—' He spread out his hands as if he could offer umpteen choices.

'Just get another drink.'

'At least,' he said when he had fetched more drink, 'we can be alone for once. I mean'—he winked—'without Brendan.'

'I thought you liked Brendan.'

'I do like him, but he's always around. We never get to talk about anything when he's around. I think that's our problem. We don't talk much about anything.'

'What's there to talk about?'

'Now and again I'd like to say something like I love you.' He broke off as if embarrassed. My mind was blank. I sat dourly as if I had been insulted. 'You hate me, don't you?' He gulped down his drink.

'I don't hate you, it's simply—'

'I know what it's simply,' he said. 'It's simply that you'd like to be shot of me.'

It was my turn to toss the drink. 'It's nobody's fault,' I said. 'I still love you. It's the life we lead. It's so pointless. All we do is drink.'

'Is there something else you want to do?' His voice was reasonable. 'Would you like to go for a walk? Or perhaps the cinema? I've two or three pounds left. Or would you like a meal? Or a box of chocolates? Just say what it is.'

I looked at my empty glass. 'Just get me another drink.'

'You know, kid,' he said, touching me under the chin, 'you're a lush. Why not admit it.'

129

'If I am,' I answered with a sardonic smile, 'it's because you made me one.'

'That's more like the girl I know and love—always blaming someone else, but it doesn't bother me. Thank God you didn't want to go to the cinema.'

'Of course I don't,' I said. 'So get me another drink.'

I don't remember clearly what happened when we got home. As usual we were the last to leave the pub. I awoke suddenly and Adam wasn't in bed. I thought I'd heard something fall. When I crept downstairs Adam was crawling round the floor like an animal or a gigantic baby, moaning and grinding his teeth and muttering words that were unintelligible. Then he shouted, 'Fire! Fire!' and began to thump the floor and weep. I turned away and crept back up to my bedroom to lie awake waiting for the dreaded creak on the stairs. It was a while since he'd been like this. I knew the war had a lot to do with it. But I had no sympathy. He should go and get treatment, but of course the first thing they'd do was tell him to keep off the drink.

*

On looking back on that particular summer it could have been described as a long hot one, or at least that is how I remember it. At the very

130

least it seemed a long one, though the end of it was swift. I could say it was the last summer I remember being happy in, though I don't think I was aware of it at the time. But when was I ever aware of being happy? It seemed then that Brendan would always be there at week-ends, irritating me, boring me, sometimes exciting me for no good reason I could think of. One evening when Adam lay on the settee in a drunken coma Brendan and I went outside and made love on the back green in the warm dark. I never reached a climax because Brendan was inept and apologetic, but I enjoyed the risk.

'Am I the only one you've done this with?' I asked him afterwards.

'No.' He fumbled with the zip on his trousers. Before I recovered from my surprise he added, 'I did it once or twice with my cousin.'

'You don't perform very well, do you?' I didn't know why I felt angry about his cousin.

'I've had too much to drink,' he said.

'I'm really quite ashamed of myself,' I said, staring up at the kids' bedroom window. 'I shouldn't be drinking at all.'

'It was all my fault,' he said. 'I took advantage of you.'

'Wouldn't it be terrible if Adam ever found out?'

'I'd kill myself if he ever found out,' said Brendan.

131

'If you're going to keep coming round we'll have to stop doing this.'

He was contrite. 'All right, but give me one last kiss.'

I allowed him to kiss my cheek. 'Was your cousin very young?'

'Sixteen. But I don't see her any more. She moved away.' He sounded ashamed.

'I'm a bit disgusted with you. A cousin? It seems incestuous somehow. Did you only do it once?'

'Don't keep on about it,' said Brendan. 'I didn't love her, like I love you.'

'Love,' I repeated, smiling in the dark. 'Tell me,' I asked, looking up at the red burning sky, 'if I got a divorce from Adam, would you marry me, and take care of the kids?'

'But I couldn't face Adam.'

'Are you frightened of him?'

He didn't answer. I pulled on his arm when he stepped forward.

'So you love me?' I followed him into the house. Adam still lay on his back with his mouth open. 'Look at him,' I said. 'If he was sick he could choke to death.'

Brendan's eyes wavered from me to Adam, his eyes far from vivid. Would you want that?'

I looked at him and laughed. 'You take everything I say far too seriously. Do you want a cup of coffee before you go?'

He followed me into the kitchen. 'I'm not coming back,' he said as he sat down on a chair and wiped the mud from the knees of his trousers, which now looked as if he'd worn them for years. I shook my head in disbelief. When he was drinking his coffee I asked him if he had started on Mr Robson's garden. He nodded. I said that was good and asked what he thought of him.

'He's all right,' said Brendan, looking into the cup.

'Does he pay you well?'

He shrugged. 'Well enough.'

'I don't know why you look so miserable. Extra money, and no worries. You've a better life than most.'

'I wish I was Adam,' he said.

'Adam? You can't mean that. He's not right in the head.'

Brendan's face relaxed. 'That makes two of us.'

'You know, Brendan,' I said, 'you'd be much happier living with Adam than with me, if it came to it.'

'You're in a funny mood tonight,' said Brendan rising. 'I think I'll go home.'

'Do that.' I swiped the coffee cups onto the floor smashing one of them. 'That's how I feel about the both of you.'

*

133

'Do you believe in God?' I asked Mrs Rossi after she had read my cards and told me that someone close was under the black shadow of death, which did not necessarily mean this person would die soon, but still the shadow was there.

'Certainly not,' she said haughtily.

'But aren't you a Jew? Didn't you imply it?'

'I didn't imply it. I implied I wasn't an Italian. But you're right. I'm a Polish Jew, though I don't like admitting it.'

'I don't blame you. They have to put up with a lot.'

'The way I see it,' said Mrs Rossi, 'they're too unsociable for my liking, and all that stuff about kosher food is very unreasonable, don't you think?' She fixed me with her black eyes as if I might disagree.

'For me it is unreasonable, but then—' I shrugged.

'Of course you gentiles have always the best of everything.'

'Catholics eat fish on a Friday,' I said.

'Sometimes they do, and sometimes they don't, but'—she spread out her hands in her fascinating continental manner—'what have kosher food and fish got to do with God?'

'Not much,' I agreed.

'It came to me one night when I was thirteen years old that there was no God. I was sitting on the steps outside the house eating a pork pie. I was very hungry you know, and I had stolen it from a baker's tray, which was a very dangerous thing to do in those days. My mother caught me when I was swallowing it down in great ecstatic gulps. She snatched what was left from my hands and stamped it into the ground. Then she pulled me by the hair into the house and locked me in the bedroom, giving me nothing to eat all night, which was a good excuse for the rest of my family to have a little extra watery soup and bread. In my room I cursed my family and God. But then as I shivered in the cold and dark it came to me in the midst of my despair that there was no God, so I merely cursed my family and felt much better.'

'What happened to your family?' I asked.

'I've no idea. I ran away from home the following year. I worked in a brothel, and did quite well all things considered. As you know, I married an Italian and eventually after many years of doing things my way, without the help of God, here I am, and as you can see, still going strong.' She laughed merrily in her infectious way and immediately I forgave her for seeing the shadow of death in my cards.

'So, my dear,' she said, wiping the tears of mirth from her eyes, 'if there is a God, which I have seen no evidence of or have had any reason to think there is, I would say God helps those who help themselves.'

'Your sentiments correspond exactly with mine, but then there was no religion in our house, apart from going to the Sunday school once a week in order to get to the Christmas party and the summer picnics.'

'There was some sense in that,' said Mrs Rossi.

We both laughed again. Poppy entered with the coffee. She looked grim. 'There's that sales fellow out there wanting to know how many letter headings you need. He looked kind of suspicious about all that screeching.'

'He can look as suspicious as he likes. Tell him I'll take fifty.'

'But we need more than that,' whined Poppy.

'Well, he'll just have to come back again when we need them.'

Poppy banged the door on her way out.

'That one is in for a surprise one day,' said Mrs Rossi.

'She does seem a bit familiar,' I said, 'but I suppose being one of the family—'

'Families are not important to me. I may just up and leave this place if I've a mind to.'

'Will you?' I said, feeling depressed. 'What about the agency?'

'You can't stay in the one place for ever, my

dear. When something tells me to move on I pay attention. I have instincts, you know, which is nothing to do with God. It is to do with—' She tapped her forehead.

Sadly I left her office, reflecting that if Mrs Rossi's agency folded up I would have to throw my lot in with Chalmers and Stroud and become permanent.

*

My encounters with Mr Robson when he gave me his letters were now as mundane as his big, sanctified room. Gone were the innuendoes and the pats. His letters became more complicated and his dictation faster. He appeared enshrouded in a surge of work, and I began to wonder about that. I ventured to ask him, 'How is Brendan suiting you?'

'Brendan?' he repeated, as if the name was foreign to him.

'The gardener,' I said with a touch of apprehension.

'Oh yes, of course, yes. He is doing his job quite well.' He stated this in a distant manner as if I had intruded into something private, then carried on with his dictation.

When he'd finished I sat up straight and said haughtily, 'About Sunday. I don't know if I can manage.'

He blinked as though I'd slapped him. 'But,

my dear, I urgently require you to come. I am on the verge of a very important discovery in my studies which may elude me if it is not set down right away.' He smiled at me ingratiatingly.

'I'll try,' I said, 'but I have a lot of things on my mind.' I added, 'Perhaps you had better get someone else.'

'But, my dear,' he said, and I was glad to see his lips quivering, 'there is no one as suitable as you.'

'How is that?'

'I thought you understood.' Now he looked pathetic.

'I am not a clairvoyant,' I said.

'But I can trust you,' he said. 'There are not many people I can trust.'

'Yes,' I said doubtfully, 'and there are not many people I can trust either when it comes to problems.'

'You can trust me.' He put his notes to one side with a slight sigh, I noticed. 'Now tell me, what is wrong?'

I proceeded to tell him, with the right degree of reluctance, that my husband was drinking heavily and we were getting into debt.

'It's not really his fault,' I concluded. 'As you know he has come through a lot; not that being in the war is a good excuse for drinking, though I can understand it in a way. But now he doesn't seem to care about anything any more. He never has any money to give me, and it's getting to the stage that I'm thinking of moving in with Brendan just to get away from it all.'

'I must say,' said Mr Robson sympathetically, 'I consider Brendan a pleasant enough fellow from what I've seen of him, but he doesn't seem very well endowed either with money or brains. How would he be any better?'

'I've thought of that too, but when one is desperate—' I broke off, biting my lower lip.

'How much do you need?' Mr Robson asked.

'It's an impossible sum. I don't want to discuss it any more.'

'Perhaps I could make a small advance.'

I confessed it was around thirty pounds, then broke down covering my face with my hands.

'Quite a bit,' he said severely, 'but if I advance you this amount will you pay me back with your Sunday earnings?'

I looked at him through grateful tears. 'Oh yes, Mr Robson. I promise I will pay.'

He dismissed me with a wave of his hand. 'Run along, my dear, and stop worrying. I'll see you on Sunday as usual.'

*

'Singing, are we?' said Adam when I arrived home clutching my plastic bag of groceries and humming 'Lili Marlene'.

139

'I hope it's not a crime.'

'No. It's nice to see you in a good mood. But I just can't help wondering what you've been up to.'

'Lamb chops, that's what I've been up to. Lamb chops for supper and a bottle for afterwards.'

Adam and the kids regarded me with blank stares.

'There's no pleasing you lot is there?'

CHAPTER EIGHT

Being an only child I should have been a lonely child, but loneliness did not afflict me in my early years, since I had two friends. Susan and Ina I called them, figments of my imagination, but very satisfactory ones for I could conjure them up at any time. I did not like Ina as much as Susan. In my mind she was always poorly dressed with a runny nose while Susan was beautiful and blonde-haired, like a doll with china-blue eyes. Susan and I whispered things about Ina, who usually walked six paces behind, pleading with us to be allowed into our company. Sometimes we let her. She was useful for games like mums and dads, or nurses and patients, when we needed a child to be slapped or a patient to be poked. Now I can see that Ina and Susan were based on myself. Susan was what I wanted to be. Ina was the real me—shy and awkward and without friends. I wonder if all lonely children play this game or only those with split personalities.

When the struggle for survival began in the primary school playground I lost trace of them altogether. I had real children to play with and yet they were always less satisfactory than my imaginary friends. It's always been like that with me. I've never taken up with anybody who is anywhere near rational. That is men, not women, for I don't rate women very highly. Adam is certainly not rational. Brendan has no intelligence whatsoever and Mr Robson is weird. But they're all I've got to work on. God helps those who help themselves, said Mrs Rossi. Perhaps she had better material to work with, or perhaps she was more skilful than me, or perhaps it is a matter of perseverance.

'I hope you are not thinking of giving your gardening job up,' I said to Brendan. The three of us were sitting in the pub.

'Did I say I was?'

'I hope you are saving some money, and not wasting it all on drink.'

'Leave him alone,' said Adam. 'He can do what he likes. It's nothing to do with you.'

'Perhaps she's right,' said Brendan, giving me the anxious eye.

'The day Betty is right we'd better all jump off a high cliff,' said Adam.

'You don't like hearing good advice?' I asked.

'Advice coming from you is dangerous, not good. I should know.'

'Since when have you ever listened to me?'

'Don't start fighting, you two,' said Brendan. He jabbed me in the side with his elbow, and I jabbed him back.

'If you like I'll put money in the post office for you,' I told him. 'Since you managed to drink before, you can still do that and save the extra.'

'I've got my suit to pay up,' said Brendan in a weak manner.

'Even with that you should still have something left.'

'You want to get your hands on Brendan's money as well,' said Adam, tapping the table with his empty glass.

'As well as what?' I asked.

'As well as the money you could paper the walls with.'

I turned to Brendan. 'Because I am trying to save a little for a holiday, which I considered would be very nice for him and the kids, he's trying to make something of it. He makes me sick.'

'Shut up and give us some money for a round,' said Adam.

When he went off to the bar I explained to Brendan, 'I'm not really going on a holiday, I'm saving to get away from him. Why don't

143

you do the same? With some money we could make plans.'

Brendan leaned back with a frightened look on his face. 'What kind of plans?'

'You exasperate me, Brendan. Without money there can be no plans. We'll both have to save up before we can make any.'

'I've never made a plan in my life,' he said with force. 'I don't feel up to it right now.'

I said very coldly, 'Don't intrude into my life then.'

'What's up with you two?' said Adam, returning to the table.

'Nothing at all,' I replied.

'I've been thinking,' said Brendan, 'if I saved up some money, I could come a holiday with you all. That is,' he said diffidently, 'if you don't mind.'

'Been at you again, has she?' said Adam.

Disdainfully I looked away. The bartender caught my eye and winked. His hair was so flat and black it was like shoe polish. He looked as if he was a guy who knew how to live it up. However, he must have received my message of not being available for the moment, for he turned his head the other way. I felt a pang of regret.

'You can forget about holidays,' I said to Brendan. 'Next year I shall be gone.'

'Begone?' repeated Adam. 'That's a good one. Begone fair maid.'

'I don't blame Betty,' said Brendan in a firm tone of voice, as though he'd done a lot of thinking about this. He gave me a conspiratorial glance.

'Who the hell are you not to blame her?' Adam spluttered over his beer, while I stared at them both as if I was watching a particularly poor play.

'She is a fine woman,' uttered Brendan, his florid face and bulky shoulders emanating the strength of a bull who spies the red cape.

'You don't say?' said Adam, fascinated. 'I've no doubt you fancy her.'

'Carry on,' I muttered to myself.

'So what,' said Brendan, flexing his shoulders. I felt a shot of admiration for him.

'Calm down,' I said, but neither of them paid any attention.

'You're getting out of hand,' said Adam, wiping the froth of beer from his mouth.

'You sneer at her far too often for my liking,' Brendan interrupted. 'You don't know how to treat women.'

Adam laughed so much he nearly fell off the seat. Heads turned to us with quizzical expressions. Adam's laughter dried up. He said to me, 'Do you, Betty, take this lump of shit to be your ever loving lover?' His voice was loud.

I decided it was time to leave. 'You can both get stuffed,' I said, and walked out with a sidelong glance at the bartender, who gave me another wink before I departed.

*

I had a phone call from Mai at work, or occupation as they preferred to call it in Chalmers and Stroud. Miss Benson's eyes were wide and curious when she handed me the receiver.

'I've managed to get something,' said Mai. 'Quite a good situation as it turns out. How about meeting me for lunch at the usual place?'

'Love to,' I said, and put the phone down.

'Was that Mai?' asked Miss Benson, standing a foot away from me.

'Mai? Oh you mean Mai. I'm not sure,' I said vaguely, walking back to my typewriter.

*

'It's really very good, and the money's a lot better,' Mai explained while I champed patiently through mashed potatoes. 'You should get out of that place,' she advised me at the end of a rambling account of her new wonder job, 'otherwise you'll become old before your time.' Her make-up was toned down a lot and her hair a lighter shade of black.

146

'I'm still working for the agency, just waiting for something better to crop up.'

'And why doesn't something crop up?'

'As a matter of fact,' I said with the air of one who has decided to come clean, 'I am in a quandary. I've been offered such a big rise by Mr Robson I don't know whether to accept it or not, but money isn't everything.'

'How much?' she asked, puckering her forehead.

I mentioned a substantial amount. Mai raised her fork to her mouth unhappily.

'I wouldn't like to work for that old creep no matter what he offered.'

'I know,' I said. 'Money's not everything. What's your boss like?'

'Very attractive and a real gentleman and good at making you feel at ease, if you know what I mean.'

'Lucky you,' I said. 'I've read of bosses like that. Unfortunately I've never met them. Perhaps if you play your cards properly—' I winked.

'Come to think of it,' said Mai, 'I wouldn't mind a night out with him, but,' she sighed, 'he's married.'

Hiding my pang of envy, though I suspected it was ill-founded, I said, 'What difference does that make?'

*

'Why don't you make love to me?' I whispered into Adam's ear. He was lying in bed with his back to me. I had figured that it was almost a fortnight since we had had sex. The contact was more necessary for me than the actual deed.

He half turned towards me. 'I can't switch on when it suits you.'

'You don't love me any more?' I asked.

'I'm not sure what I feel about you,' he grumbled softly.

'Neither am I sure about you.'

'You're very devious,' he said, stroking my hair.

'My mother used to say I was too deep for her liking.'

'Forget your mother.' Our arms were touching now. 'I don't want anyone else, that's for sure.'

I smiled, staring up at the ceiling.

'I suppose I'm difficult to live with. It's not been easy for you,' he said.

'It's not been easy for you either.' Our voices sounded wooden, like the first stages of a prayer meeting.

'In what way?' he asked.

'Perhaps the war—' I began.

'I drink too much,' he said.

'So do I.' Now we were facing, but it was dark. He was like a stranger. 'We don't drink

148

all that much.' I stroked his cheek. It was like a stranger's cheek.

'I'm thinking of giving it up,' he said.

'Sex?'

He laughed, like a stranger. 'I thought I had. I mean drink.'

'The kids would miss it; I mean us stopping the drink. They wouldn't recognise us.'

'What a terrible thing to say.' He was now stroking my breast, which strangely enough I couldn't stand. It made me feel as if I was being insulted or assaulted, unlike any other part of my body.

'We could make it up to them by buying lots of fancy gear.'

'Or holidays,' he added.

'They'd likely prefer us to drink on holidays, otherwise we'd be no fun.'

'One thing,' he said, squeezing my nipple, which made me want to scream. 'Without drink Brendan would vanish like the proverbial rose of yester-year.'

'You're not jealous of Brendan, by any chance?' I asked.

He withdrew his hand, saying, 'Should I be?'

'You're such a fool, Adam,' I said. 'You deliberately encourage him, make him feel as if we were his foster-parents, then for no good reason want to get rid of him.'

Adam moved round and lay straight on his back with one arm under his head. 'We have drifted into a situation with Brendan which frankly is getting on my nerves.'

'He's like a child, isn't he? I don't know what to do about him either.'

Adam gave one long sigh. 'Fuck Brendan,' he said. Roughly he pulled me close then moved on top of me.

'Fuck me,' I said. Normally I don't like the word, but I was excited.

Afterwards Adam said quietly and sincerely, 'No more drink then?'

'Right,' I said, wishing I could have one long pull on a bottle of wine to set me off to sleep. The act had done nothing for me.

*

On Sunday when I was in Mr Robson's kitchenette I noticed there were two five-pound notes lying under the coffee jar. I looked quickly away and asked him if I should pour.

'Please do,' he said as he laid an embroidered linen square under my cup.

'That's pretty,' I remarked.

'My wife was a beautiful stitcher,' he said.

I looked through the window at a patch of upturned earth. 'I noticed Brendan has been busy,' I said.

'He has uprooted some of my plants,' said

Mr Robson darkly, 'but I don't think he will do it again.'

'Perhaps he's not suitable.'

'He's careless, but I think he's learned his lesson.'

'Lesson?' I repeated stupidly.

'Don't worry, my dear, Brendan and I understand one another. He's not a complicated person, but let's say being acquainted with the criminal mind I have a way of talking to him.'

'Brendan's not a criminal,' I said, putting my cup down on the saucer with a clatter.

'I shouldn't think so, but he has a behaviour pattern which could be associated with crime. He interests me.'

'I'm surprised to hear this, Mr Robson. I certainly would not have spoken for anyone if I'd thought they were the criminal type.'

'I'm sure you wouldn't, my dear. What I should have said is that Brendan is the kind who has a direct approach to life, a simple type who views situations in black and white rather than in various shades of grey like you and I. But let's not worry about him,' he said hurriedly. 'There is much to be done.'

The notes headed 'Capabilities of Human Behaviour in Animals' were spiced with a lot of jargon I could not understand. Some parts that I could understand held my attention for seconds, but I mainly plodded through it with a feeling of boredom and a feeling that Mr Robson, though not exactly crazy, was very eccentric. When I visited his toilet at one point in the day I noticed for the first time a small circular hole above the cistern. Viciously I plugged it with an old biscuit wrapper from my pocket. Later I followed him up to the bedroom, reassured by the fragile set of his shoulders and the way he tottered like an old man uncertain of his footsteps.

'I fear you may think this is all very strange,' he murmured when I was seated in front of the mirror of his dressing-table, 'but you understand I don't require you to do anything other than—' He broke off.

'Yes,' I said, staring at my pale, strained reflection in the mirror.

'Now my dear, just undress very slowly while I go behind the screen. As you know it's the only way I can—'

'Yes, I know,' I said sighing, thinking at least he might have heated up the room.

He coughed and vanished behind the screen.

On the way out I picked up the two fivers lying under the coffee jar.

'Is this . . .?' I said, waving them in front of his face.

'It is, it is,' he said, nodding his head as if he had discovered more human behaviour in animals.

*

'Can't you get me something else?' I asked Mrs Rossi. 'I'm not keen on my situation now. Frankly I can't stand Mr Robson. He is very difficult.'

'Most people are,' she said, languidly popping a dark chocolate into her mouth. She offered me the box. Impatiently I waved it away.

'He's crazy,' I said, adding, 'possibly worse than crazy.'

'But generous,' she said.

'He's sick,' I pointed out.

'But generous,' she said again.

'He's a creep, maybe dangerous.'

'You'll not get a better position,' she said, putting the chocolates back in the drawer, and feeling about in it as if looking for something.

'Don't bother with the cards,' I said. 'I've no time to spare.'

'Other than that I can't help you,' she said. 'Besides, I'm winding up all my affairs. I'm tired of living in this country. People are not interested in the occult. They'd rather believe in God and all that rubbish.'

'Fortune telling doesn't sound too secure,' I agreed.

'I'm tired of security. Death is preferable at times.'

'I know how you feel,' I said. 'I thought money might be a good reason for sticking to

Mr Robson, but I can't stand it when he goes behind the screen. He's old and he smells.'

'Behind the screen?' Her eyes shone blackly and she laughed. 'What does he do?'

'I don't know but I have my suspicions.' We both laughed at that.

'I knew him quite well when I was younger,' she said, wiping her eyes.

'Nowadays he studies human behaviour in animals.'

'Don't tell me any more,' said Mrs Rossi, now holding her heaving sides. 'I'll do myself an injury.'

'But you see what I mean,' I said after she'd calmed down and brought out her long cigarette holder. 'I'm still young and it's no life for a working mother.'

Mrs Rossi's laughter was threatening to surge up again.

'Look,' I said, 'can't you find me something to do in the fortune telling line? I could be your receptionist.'

'I've got Poppy for that.'

I hung my head despairingly. 'That's that then,' I said.

'Wouldn't you like to try the cards?' she asked. 'They might help.'

'If the future is so certain, I can't do anything about it.'

'True,' she agreed. 'Listen,' she said suddenly.

154

'I'll see what I can do for you once I get established somewhere else. Meanwhile throw in your lot with Mr Robson. He's generous and not such a bad old stick really. He might snuff it and leave you a fortune.'

CHAPTER NINE

'How much have I got now?' Brendan asked as he handed over two pounds for me to put into my savings account in the post office.

'You mean how much have we got,' I corrected him. 'Well, between you and me we have seven pounds ten shillings.'

He was sitting with his elbows on the kitchen table, hands cupping his face. 'Not bad,' he said, looking impressed.

'I think it's wonderful,' I said, tying a chiffon scarf on the side of my neck. 'How do I look?'

'Stunning. What's it for anyway?'

'My scarf?'

'The money.'

In a low voice I said, 'I get so tired of you at times. I've to keep explaining things. You remind me of that Lennie guy in *Of Mice and Men*.'

'What guy's that?' He brought his arms off the table and stared at me wildly.

'Look, when we get enough we can set up some little business between us. There's this woman I know. She's marvellous at telling fortunes and that's something that people are always keen on hearing. But she needs some capital to rent a good place, and a couple of assistants for various duties—'

'I thought you said we were going a holiday; me, you and Adam.'

'I think I'll give you your money back. I see it's no use.'

He stood up and grabbed my hand. 'Please don't. I'm really all for going into business.'

I kissed his forehead, which was damp. Brendan sweats a lot, probably because of his weight. 'Before you do that,' I said, 'you'll have to get your hair cut and your suit cleaned. It's full of stains.'

I stopped talking when Adam came into the kitchen rubbing his hands, his face nicely pink from shaving. Compared to Brendan he looked admirable.

'All ready I hope.' He beamed. Arm-in-arm we sauntered down to the pub as jolly as the three musketeers.

*

On Sunday morning I opened my eyes with the

157

sensation they had been stuck together with paste. Adam lay face down on the pillow making gurgling noises. I glanced despairingly at the alarm clock and pulled the sheet over my head. Then the kids came in and sat on top of us, jumping up and down as if they were on ponies.

'We want breakfast,' shouted Rae.

Adam lifted his head and croaked, 'Go and fry some sausages.'

I considered pleading a terminal illness, but Mr Robson hovered on my mind like the peal of a church bell to the faithful.

'Last time we made sausages they got burnt,' declared Robert.

'Only on the outside,' I said. 'Inside they were raw.' I addressed Adam's back. 'Why can't you make the breakfast? You're not doing anything else.'

'Apart from the washing, the ironing, the cooking and the cleaning.'

'Not the ironing,' I said, adding gently, 'You know I've to go out and earn money.'

'For doing what? That's what I'd like to know.'

'Is Mr Robson a nice man?' Rae asked, most inappropriately.

'Not particularly, but he gives me money for typing.'

Adam laughed like a dog barking. 'Don't

158

believe a word of what she says.'

'Can we have some?' asked Rae.

'Go and make cornflakes and I'll give you a shilling each.'

They scampered off. Adam turned round and said, looking dangerous, 'All this money you earn, we don't seem to be any better off. What do you do with it?'

I closed my eyes and clasped my hands as if praying. 'I am saving up.'

'For what?'

'Because,' I said carefully, as if he was a child who did not take things in easily, 'I am going to start a business, if you must know.' Hastily I swung my legs out of the bed and donned an old coat which I used as a dressing-gown.

'Business?' He sat bolt upright. I half expected his hair to stand on end.

'Yes, business,' I repeated, relieved that I had uttered the word.

He jumped out of bed and grabbed the front of my raincoat as if I had said something vile. 'What the hell are you up to?'

'Calm yourself,' I said. 'It was to be a secret. I was going to tell you once I got the thing going. I have plans for us, great plans really, but I might have known you wouldn't understand.'

'You're mad,' he said, and threw himself back on the bed looking exhausted.

'So that's why I work through the week and

159

on Sundays: to save money.'

'What kind of business?' he asked listlessly.

'You'll never believe it,' I laughed, dressing rapidly at the same time.

'Try me.'

'Remember that woman Mai who came out to the pub not so long ago?'

'The one that looked like a whore?'

'Really, Adam. She's a nice, sensible person, who had too much make-up on, that's all.'

'Go on—about the business.'

'Well. I hope you are listening closely.'

He nodded his head. His mouth looked slack.

'The lady at the agency, Mrs Rossi, you've heard me mention her—'

He shook his head and closed his eyes.

'And myself, and Mai, are all going into the agency line—'

'Call girls?'

Ignoring this, I continued. 'Mrs Rossi wants to expand but she needs two more partners like Mai and myself.' My brain couldn't invent any more, so I finished off by saying, 'Take it or leave it, Adam, but I've got ambitions and I don't want you standing in my way.'

'Right,' he said, 'that's fine.' He yawned. I thought he looked pale. When I left the room he called, 'I too have my ambitions. I'll be gone when you return.'

160

I shook my head and looked at him sympathetically. I had heard it all before.

*

Not being in much of a hurry to encounter Mr
Robson I dallied on his garden path, admiring
the fuchsias, rhododendrons, roses and other
blooms with the uneasy feeling that Mr Robson
could be peering through the net curtains. I
spent another five minutes round the back of the
house staring at reddish-brown upturned earth
where apparently Brendan had been digging. I
admitted it did nothing for the look of the
place, but no doubt there was a reason for it. I
saw a string vest hanging on the washing-line,
harmless but suggestive of Mr Robson's old
body. I shook my head to cancel the image and
knocked hard on the backdoor. It was ajar, so
I entered. In the kitchen I ran my hand along
the marble table-top alongside the sink unit and
touched the silk lacy curtains on the window. I
opened the cupboard above the sink unit and
took down two cups and saucers, in readiness
for the coffee. Then I decided I had gone far
enough with Mr Robson's utensils so I waited
for him, sitting on the kitchen stool. After five
minutes I called, 'Mr Robson—I have arrived.'
I tip-toed into the large room where I studied
the photographs on the wall, particularly the
steadfast face of the hanged man, but my mind

was distracted by the absence of my employer. I left the room and climbed up the stairs to Mr Robson's bedroom, calling, 'Are you there, Mr Robson?' I entered the unoccupied room, was unable to resist looking behind the screen, but found nothing more than a desk with some sheets of paper. 'Mr Robson!' I called again, and picked up a sheet which was marked with my name. I read the contents with a sense of surprise, relief and anger. This was due to one paragraph which said, 'It would appear that this subject is a reckless young woman who will readily enter into a situation without any thought of consequences. Given certain factors she could be a danger to society. Without any qualms she sits on the other side of the screen with an air of expectation which would be frightening if it were not so interesting. Such simple tests have proved—'

I stopped reading when I heard a noise from below, but on running downstairs into the kitchen I found a draught had caused the door to bang. I closed it forcefully. The activities of this deluded old man made me want to puke. It seemed I had displayed my soul to him for a few paltry pounds. On the way back home I calmed down. There was no harm done really. I would display a lot more than that if the price was right. That's how desperate I had become.

Adam's bed was unmade. The kids' room

looked as if it had been burgled with all the drawers left open. Spilled cornflakes littered the carpet. Downstairs on top of the radio I found an envelope. The message inside read:

'Good-bye, Betty. Have taken the kids with me. Sorry things didn't work out. Hope you succeed with your business arrangements.'

My first reaction was shock, then anger, then relief. I could now do what I wanted without Adam breathing down my neck. I expected he would leave the kids with his stepmother, who'd be glad to take them in. She always spoiled them rotten whenever she got the chance. 'Poor neglected lambs' she described them. My main problem was how to get in touch with Brendan. He never usually showed up on Sundays.

*

On Monday morning Mr Robson did not appear.

'Any word from him?' I asked Miss Benson. 'He wasn't at home on Sunday when I called to do his typing.'

'Ah yes, your typing,' she said, smiling mysteriously. 'No, we have heard nothing.'

I sat around all morning, yawning and filing my nails with my neat little manicure set. I offered to do some typing for one of the other women for the sake of passing the time. This offer was refused. I became keenly miserable about everything. I pined for Mr Robson's return or for a sign he would be back. At lunch-time I was thankful to see Mai inside the coffee bar. She listened to me with an air of abstraction when I told her about Mr Robson.

'Probably has the flu and can't be bothered phoning,' she said.

'But he wasn't around on Sunday.'

'Perhaps he decided to take a holiday.'

'Could be,' I said. After that we had nothing much to say. Suddenly we'd become strangers with only the weather to talk about.

'I meant to tell you,' she said when we had moved out onto the street. 'I've had my lunch-time altered. Can't say when I'll see you again, but I'll give you a ring.'

'Yes, do that,' I said in a similar distracted manner before I caught the bus back.

*

I'm looking over the veranda of the cottage hospital to where a bus shelter stands covered in graffiti. I can make out the words 'Fuck the Pope'. Lady Lipton is asleep. She's been asleep for most of my tale. I'm surprised when she says with her eyes still closed, 'Is that all?'

'All what?' I said, wishing I was sitting in

the bus shelter talking to some wino with a bottle to share.

'You said you caught the bus back. What happened after that?'

'Weren't you listening?'

'I heard most of it, though I may have dozed off at the boring parts. Please do go on.'

'It's not true anyway,' I said off-handedly.

'It sounds to me like a whodunit where you have to plough through a lot of red herrings before it gets to the point. Believe me I've got a pile of them in my locker and I know the set-up off by heart. So what happened after you caught the bus? I suppose your husband and children returned and Mr Robson wrote you a letter to say he didn't require your services any more. Is that it?'

'I never saw Mr Robson again. And as a matter of fact my husband's got another woman.'

My hand tightened on the rail of the veranda. I wondered if I should jump over and land with a splatter on the street below. On the other hand the railings were too high for me to climb. This was a pity I thought at that moment. I turned away from the old woman. I'd said enough.

*

I stayed away from Chalmers and Stroud to allow Mr Robson plenty of time to worry about

165

me. At home I washed and polished everything I could lay my hands on, appreciating the peace and quiet of the house as well as the money I saved on food now Adam and the kids were gone. There was no loneliness in the double bed at night. I could stretch and toss and turn without encountering Adam's stiff animosity. It was like a holiday when the sun shone through clean bedroom windows in the morning. The kitchen too had an unfamiliar foreign look about it: tidy and tasteful with a bunch of stolen roses from the garden next door on the centre of the table, while I daintily munched toast and marmalade for my breakfast. Later I remember a fine drizzle of rain as I went to the post office and lifted some money from the savings account. The first blow fell when I called round at Mrs Rossi's and found the door locked. I rattled and banged to no avail. A man came out on the landing below and shouted, 'Don't you know she's scarpered?' and added, 'Funny business!' in a questioning way.

I walked down to him and said, knowing it would be useless, 'Any idea where she's gone?'

He shook his head. 'Owes you money does she?' Then without waiting for an answer he went back inside.

I was sad about Mrs Rossi's departure, unlike Adam's and the kids', which at the

166

time I thought was only temporary. I called at Chalmers and Stroud to be told by an excited Miss Benson that they had heard nothing from Mr Robson, though this was not unusual since he was known to go off to foreign holiday resorts whenever he took the urge.

'Very inconvenient for you I suppose,' she said, her voice thinly insincere.

'That's all right,' I said. 'I don't mind the rest.'

'I'll let you know when he gets back, but—'

'I've no doubt he'll let me know himself,' I said, giving her a wave.

*

Brendan appeared just after I had shovelled most of my meal of tinned tuna and beetroot into the dustbin, replacing it with a glass of vodka. He followed me into the kitchen. I told him to sit down and poured him a glass. He drank it over as if it was water.

'That's vodka and lemonade,' I informed him.

He nodded, wiped his mouth, looked behind him in a troubled way and said, 'Very nice. Can I have another one?'

'Don't be so greedy.' But I refilled his glass and mine, adding a splash of lemonade. The hand reaching out for it was dirty, his finger-nails engrained. 'You're a mess, Brendan,' I

167

said. 'Worse than usual. You might have washed.'

He stared at me as if I was speaking in a foreign language.

'By the way,' I said loudly as if he was deaf, 'Adam's gone.'

'Gone where?'

'Left days ago. Took the kids with him.'

There was a noise from Brendan's throat which could have been a hiccup or a sob. His face crumpled and he cried like a child.

'For God's sake, it's me he's left, not you.'

'What will I do?' he wailed, pressing his face on the table.

'Have another drink, that's what.' I surveyed his bowed head with disgust. 'Go and wash yourself and brush that suit. It looks as if you've been sleeping in a byre with it on. We might as well go out and enjoy ourselves.'

Brendan looked up, his eyes like small pools of mud. 'It's not the same without Adam.'

'I agree, but since I've been alone in this place all week I want out.' I hauled him off the chair and shoved him into the bathroom. It definitely was not the same without Adam, but that would pass. Freedom was the thing.

I felt much more optimistic in the pub, being squiffy from the vodka we already had. Brendan was giggling now.

'Alone at last,' I said, trying to match his continual vivid-blue stares.

'Here's to Adam.' He held up his glass squintily, spilling some of the drink.

'Tell me,' I said after some more desultory talk, 'what's happened to Mr Robson?'

'Who's that?' He giggled uncontrollably.

'You're drunk,' I said.

He wagged his finger close to my nose. 'You're beautiful. Will you marry me?'

'You're a fool,' I said, warming to his fatuous, beaming face, 'but I'll always love you.' I traced a cross on his forehead. 'What about Mr Robson though?'

'Fuck the old bastard, that's what I say.'

I was impressed by the touch of violence. 'You're dead right. He owes me money.'

'Don't worry about money. Look!' He showed me a ten-pound note. 'I've got more where that came from.'

It was a pretty sight. I'd never felt so happy as I did at that moment. I was like Irma la Douce finding her true lover. 'Tomorrow we will go to the seaside,' I said, 'and sit outside a hotel at a table with an umbrella, and sip Martini.'

'And we can go to the races and back horses,' said Brendan excitedly.

'While I watch through binoculars,' I added. We held hands and made outrageous plans,

169

laughing aloud. The barman came over and wiped our table.

'Where's Adam?' he asked reprovingly.

'Gone,' I said.

'Gone with the wind,' Brendan added, now almost hysterical.

'Take it easy with the drink,' said the barman. 'I don't want to have to put you out.'

I winked at him. 'It's Brendan's birthday. We're just celebrating.'

The barman walked away, looking as if he'd rather hear no more about it. Brendan's mood changed. 'I hope he comes back,' he said anxiously. Two drinks later he was crying.

'Let's go,' I said when I saw the barman staring over. Passing the licensed grocer's I purchased some sweet wine. Every so often I had to return and drag Brendan along the road. Like a dog he was wavering at every lamp-post. Inside the house I had a drink while he was sick in the toilet. After that he sat in Adam's chair, pale and lumpy and unhappy.

'Go to bed,' I said. He lumbered off like a wounded bear. There was a lot of crashing on the stairs, but I couldn't be bothered to investigate. No news was good news the ways things were going. After that I let down the pulley and began to fold up the clothes—a skirt of Rae's, a shirt of Robert's, and some socks of Adam's. In a drunken, dramatic way,

I said aloud, 'This is all that remains of my family,' then I drank some more wine with the happier thought that tomorrow Brendan and I would go to the seaside. On Monday I would search for Adam and the kids and we would all start afresh. Clearly it was impossible for me to pass the rest of my life with Brendan. I discovered him later sprawled across the bed with his clothes on. He had not even taken off his boots. I tried to push him over to get under the covers, but he was as heavy as an ox. I staggered into the kids' room and lay down on Rae's bed, falling asleep with the smell of Johnson's shampoo, which a friend had given her for her birthday.

On Saturday I awoke feeling uneasy. I looked at the small Walt Disney clock on Rae's set of drawers. Half past one, it read. Surely it had stopped. I held it to my ear and in disbelief listened to the steady tick tick. 'Brendan!' I shouted, rushing through to my room, surprised that I had all my clothes on. Apart from rumpled blankets and a dirty smear on the bedcover there was no sign of him. 'Don't leave me, Brendan,' I sobbed, nearly falling down the stairs to reach the kitchen, but I knew he wouldn't be there. The front door was slightly open. He couldn't even shut it properly, I thought bitterly. I drank coffee while I tried to figure everything out. It was like a badly produced film where you try to put two and two together, knowing that the murderer is the one you least suspect, while thinking the script writer must be crazy because the plot is so bad. The fact was that all the people I was connected with were disappearing. I thought I'd better start praying for them to come back, but that seemed like giving in or going against my principles. Besides, maybe Brendan had gone home to change for the outing. 'We can go to the races,' he had said, though I couldn't see him worrying about appearance. Anyway, he had very little to change with. Perhaps he was merely checking in with his mother. Perhaps this, perhaps that. I took off my crumpled dress, washed my face, and sat around in my underskirt waiting for him to return, as there was nothing else to do but finish the remainder of the wine facing me on the table. This took the edge off things. It was clammily hot. I would have liked to lie down on the grass in the back green. Instead I lay on the settee in the living-room singing snatches of songs like 'See What the Boys in the Back Room Will Have', and 'The Isle of Capri'. I had conversations with people like Adam and Mrs Rossi, who were with me in spirit if not in reality. I actually had a good time before I fell asleep, hearing in my head Brendan sing, 'Gwine to run all night, gwine to run all day,

I'll bet my money on de bobtail nag—' He does have a humour of a kind, I thought drowsily.

*

I can't remember too much of the rest of the week-end, but I must have dressed later on in the evening and fetched another bottle from the licensed grocer's. I have a vague recollection of sitting in the back green in the dusk with the rain cooling my forehead. I think I was very happy until the man next door loomed up in front of me. 'Mind your own business,' I said, but sensing trouble I withdrew indoors clutching the bottle. I slept most of Sunday but was forced up by a blinding thirst for water. In the shadows of the kitchen I groped to the tap and realised I was completely alone.

CHAPTER TEN

I gave Lady Lipton a nudge. She was nodding off again.

'Do you hear what I said,' I shouted in her ear. 'I was completely alone.'

She jumped a bit and said, 'Because I am closing my eyes does not mean I haven't been following what you say. I find this Brendan fellow very drab. I don't know what you saw in him. I'm more interested in Mr Robson, a strange fellow perhaps, but at least he had some kind of breeding. What became of him?'

'Ah, Mr Robson,' I said, smiling. 'I'll come to that. All in good time.' I leaned back in the chair and shut my eyes, rocking myself to and fro.

She nipped my arm painfully. 'So what became of him?'

'Well—' I paused once again. My head felt almost worn out by the details of what was history to me now.

'Come on,' she said, her skinny fingers reaching out for another nip. I went on.

*

After that things became a bit hazy. For a week I remained in the house, sozzled most of the time. I had enough money in the savings account to buy drink. I don't remember eating. Again I was having a good time. They all came in and listened to me. They never did much talking, being only there in my mind. But they listened; Adam, Brendan, Mr Robson, sometimes Mai and Mrs Rossi. I admit I was probably off my rocker. I'm certain Adam came back once in reality. As usual he was shouting various accusations, and I pulled a blanket over my head to shut out the voice. Finally a social worker came. I believe I have him to thank for that, the swine.

When he visited me later in here he sat on the edge of the bed examining his finger-nails. I told him he didn't look well and asked if he was still drinking.

'Not really,' he answered. 'Perhaps that's why I don't look well.'

'I feel marvellous,' I said, struggling to sit

up. I looked down at the rough white hospital nightdress and told him when he came next time to bring me a decent one.

He said, 'Have you got any? I don't remember you ever wearing one.'

I told him for God's sake to buy one, and asked if he didn't care how I looked.

'I'll get you one,' he said quickly.

I asked how the kids were.

'Happy.' He looked away, as if he could not stand the sight of me.

I asked how he was managing without me and he said, 'Very well.' I said that I hoped he was keeping everything tidy, as I had left the house very clean.

He looked at me so miserably that I yearned to forgive him, then he said the house was no longer his responsibility, and, 'It's over a month since I left you. Don't you remember?'

'Oh,' I said, 'how time flies.'

After a long pause I asked why he had come to see me. He said because I had been very ill and was the mother of his children. I laughed, which hurt my chest a bit.

'The mother of your children! That sounds like the pen of my aunt. We got that in French at school.'

'I never took French,' he said with the martyred look he had on his face the day

176

he came home from the war and passed our window.

'Welcome home, Adam,' I said.

He took this literally. He said, 'It's no use, Betty. I'm not coming back. I'm not saying it was all your fault, but after what's happened I couldn't face it.'

'Fuck you,' I said and closed my eyes. The bed creaked as he lifted his weight off. I opened my eyes, aware he was about to leave.

'What happened anyway? I got drunk for a time. So what's the big deal?'

'The big deal is'—his eyes bored into mine— 'that Brendan has been arrested for murder.'

I closed my eyes to hide the shock and said I was not surprised.

'Aren't you the clever one?' said Adam. 'You're not surprised. Did you arrange it like you arranged everything else?'

I shook my head. I was too tired to argue. I wanted him to go. He reached out and gripped my wrist hard. It was painful.

He said, 'You put it into his head to work for Robson.'

I told him it was only a suggestion.

'And the money he saved on your suggestion, what happened to that?'

I told him I had drunk it, which was why

I was in here, and to let go because he was hurting me. He released me with a look of contempt, or hatred, or both.

'So he murdered Mr Robson,' I said, putting my hands under the blankets as they had become very cold.

He said, 'And you gave him the idea.'

I told him to go away as I couldn't think properly. He stood up looking like an apparition. Could I be dreaming all this, I wondered. But no.

He said, 'It was a nasty business. He smashed Robson on the side of the head with a spade. The body was scarcely recognisable when they found it in the garden shed. Doesn't that shock you?'

'I'll think about it later,' I promised. 'Just go away or I'll ring the bell for the nurse.'

I buried my face in the pillow listening to the sound of his receding footsteps. When the nurse came I asked for a sleeping pill. She said, 'Not now, dear,' so I told her to get my clothes, that I was not stopping here, that I must have a drink, that my husband always upset me. Finally she gave me something in a glass.

'Promise you won't let any visitors in again,' I said, 'especially him. It's because of him I'm in here. I like it here. I wish I could stay here for ever.'

The nurses appear to like me, perhaps because I take their pills without any bother. I'm not one of those who complain, saying we're being turned into junkies. I don't care. I like helping to hand round tea and scones before climbing into bed for the afternoon snooze. It's a lovely feeling. In the evening before they dim the lights the pills give me a nice woozy, relaxed sensation like a good gargle of wine. This is one of the best times I ever had.

*

Today Lady Lipton appears to be in a trance. Her eyes are open but unblinking. I move my hand up and down in front of her face.

'Don't do that, you bitch,' she says.

'I thought you were in a state of coma.'

'I was merely thinking that the tea was late.'

'Is that all you were thinking?'

'Actually no. Did you really encourage that Brendan fellow to kill Mr Robson?'

'As a matter of fact I didn't,' I snapped. 'What use was Mr Robson to me dead?'

'Revenge perhaps?'

'Revenge for what? Jesus Christ, he wasn't my lover.'

'People can lie,' she said, giving me a withering glance.

'That's true. I don't believe you are a lady.'

179

'It doesn't matter what you believe,' she said. 'It's what's in my head that counts, and I know it's true.'

'So, you were one of the upper class?' I sneered.

'Near enough, when I look back on it. It was only after my husband died everything went wrong.'

'You mean when you took to the bottle?'

'If you like to put it that way,' she said, her face untroubled. 'But I had my good times,' she added.

'Adam once said to me we were put into this world to look at a picture, and it was up to us whether we liked it or not. But,' I added, 'the picture he got was one of war. He was a disturbed man.'

She stared at me with a glance of incomprehension. At that moment a nurse came forward with tea and fairy cakes. 'Here you are, dears,' she said with a charitable smile.

When she turned away I gave her the two-finger sign.

'You're very rude,' said Lady Lipton, shoving a tiny cake into her mouth. It made her choke. 'Oh dear,' she said when she regained her breath, 'I can't seem to swallow properly nowadays.' In the same breath she asked, 'Did they hang Brendan?'

'Capital punishment has been abolished.

180

Besides, the lawyer put forward a case of diminished responsibility.'

'It makes me sick to think of all the thugs going around. There's no decency in the young people nowadays.'

'Brendan wasn't that young. Over twenty he was. And you didn't know Mr Robson.'

'From what you say he was a gentleman, eccentric I dare say, but a gentleman for all that.'

'Have my fairy cake,' I said. 'It's a bit stale. But not so much you'd notice.'

'I suppose you will visit him in jail.'

'Of course not. Why should I?'

'Weren't you fond of him? I thought he was your boy-friend.'

'Brendan?' I laughed. 'He was so stupid he was no use to anyone, not even himself. It was because of him Adam left me. I could never forgive him for that.'

'It couldn't have been all his fault,' said Lady Lipton, 'if your husband was carrying on with another woman. He would have left you in any case.'

I became so angry that I shook her by the shoulder. 'How do you know what he would have done? Supposing I told you I made the whole thing up?'

'Then why are you so angry?' she said, rubbing her arm without any look of pain.

181

'Only some of it's true,' I said, regretting having opened my mouth. 'I am married to a man called Adam, who had a pal Brendan. He happened to kiss me one day when Adam was out of the room, nothing more than that. I didn't fancy him, he was so awful. But he died a long time ago in very dull circumstances.'

'Was there no Mr Robson?'

'Oh yes, but'—I shrugged—'he was a dotary old lawyer who I typed for now and again. That was all. And while I'm at it, Mrs Rossi did not tell fortunes. In fact I don't think the woman who ran the agency was called Mrs Rossi; something like Smith or Brown.'

Lady Lipton looked doubtful. 'It seems to me you don't know what the truth is. From now on I won't believe a single word you say.'

'And you'll be right,' I said, finishing off the sweet, milky tea. 'When you're in here everything gets so jumbled up it's hard to know the truth.'

'I know what you mean. I can scarcely remember what the estate looked like, but I dream about it.'

'I never dream about anything.'

'Not even your children?'

'Not even my children,' I told her, with a hard stare.

'Oh well,' she said, 'it's time for our rest soon, thank God. I'm worn out with all this chatter. Talk, talk, all talk. I would give anything to be back home on my estate, but—' She threw her hands up in the air in a delicate manner, then rose and walked back into the ward.

*

It must have been about a fortnight after Brendan disappeared that the social worker called.

'How are you keeping, dear?' she asked.

'Fine,' I said. 'But I've no money and nothing to eat unless you count some blue-moulded bread and potatoes with shoots growing out of them.'

She gave me three pounds, explaining that it would be deducted from any money the Social Security might allow me. I listened to all this with a sense of despondency, then I asked if there was any chance of me getting the kids back since I didn't trust my husband to take care of them properly. When she looked at me doubtfully I explained that he had been in the war and was not responsible for himself, let alone children. I tapped the side of my head to give her a clearer picture of him, but all she said was that she'd make enquiries. Meanwhile, she added, the best thing for me to do was to take it

183

easy and not worry myself too much about anything. She was sure the children would be all right. The important point was that I attend the clinic on the date stipulated on the card.

'Nonsense,' I said. 'There is nothing wrong with me. I simply had too much to drink. But I'm all right now.'

'That's fine, dear, but I still think you should attend the clinic if you want to get back on your feet.'

'I am back on my feet!' I shouted. 'I want you to find out where my husband and kids are! I want them home!'

'That,' she said firmly, 'is not to be considered at present.'

I told her to fuck off. After she had left with a tightened mouth I looked out my Robin Hood suit, as Adam called it, applied some make-up and headed for the licensed grocer's. I was careful with the money, only purchasing a half-bottle to help me think about what I was going to do.

*

About a week later, which seemed like a month, I spied Adam pushing a trolley along the Co-operative floor. Mai was with him putting tins into it. They both looked cheerful until they saw me.

'Adam,' I said, confronting him and wondering why Mai of all people should be helping him with the shopping.

He looked at me woodenly but said nothing.

'I'm not working any more,' I explained gaily, winking at Mai. In a way it was good to see her. She would back me up and take the edge of Adam's truculent mood.

'I'm glad to see you looking so well,' he said at last.

'Please forgive me,' I said with a catch in my voice.

'I forgive you.'

'Has Mai'—I gave her a look of gratitude—'been looking after you then?'

Mai responded glumly, 'You could say that.'

'Look, Mai,' I said, 'could you leave us alone for a few minutes. It's not going to be easy—'

'Mai is staying where she is.'

A twitch came into my eye which I found embarrassing.

'You mean you two are—' I stopped, strangely surprised. She wasn't his type.

'Yes, we are,' said Adam, looking over my head.

'Are what?' I wanted to stamp my feet and spit on them both.

'Going to get married once Adam gets the

185

divorce,' said Mai, searching his face as she spoke.

'You can't,' I shrieked. 'He's a nut case. I'm the only one who understands him.'

'I'm afraid we'll have to go now,' said Adam politely, as though he was talking to a Jehovah's Witness.

'Yes, the kids will be wondering where we are,' said Mai. 'We don't like to leave them too long on their own.'

They both turned and practically ran out the Co-operative. Adam was carrying the shopping bag. I wondered if there was drink in it. I felt like shouting, 'You bastard. You never carried shopping bags for me.'

They were gone when I got outside. It was raining again. Without thinking, I brought out from my plastic bag the bottle of sherry which I had just bought, unscrewed the top and took a long swallow. After that everything was a blur in my head.

*

Lady Lipton said I was in a bad state when they brought me in, shouting and scream-ing and acting like a madwoman. I don't particularly believe her. She's the type that exaggerates. But I put up with her. She's the only one worth talking to in here. I haven't seen Adam since he told me about Brendan.

186

You'd think he'd come and visit me now and again and bring the kids. It would be nice for us to be together again. After all, I am their mother.

A NOTE ON THE AUTHOR

Agnes Owens is the author of the novels
Gentlemen of the West and *Birds in the
Wilderness* and contributed short stories to
the collection *Lean Tales* which also includes
stories by James Kelman and Alasdair Gray.